PRAISE FOR CYNTHIA ROGERSON

'Cynthia Rogerson is a new writer of great clarity and humanity – definitely one to watch.'
A.L. Kennedy

'Her writing has a lovely spirit to it; an appealing mixture of the spiky and the warm.'
Michel Faber

'A witty, sharp, touching novel full of fine observation, sparkling dialogue and moments of quiet depth.'
James Robertson

'Cynthia Rogerson's four narrators are very different from each other, but they are each equally desperate and equally beguiling. These four characters in search of love captured me from the first and kept me reading until the end. *I Love You, Goodbye* is a hugely accomplished novel and Rogerson is an author with a future. This is an original piece of work which deserves a wide readership.'
Louise Welsh

'What is love? Love is the relationship that will develop between you and this quirky, wise and fascinating novel. Your heart will pang with recognition again and again as Rogerson explores the foibles that make relationships so beautiful and so heartbreaking. An engaging, insightful and witty novel that resonates with a profound emotional intelligence.'
Kevin MacNeil

'I've just finished reading *I Love You, Goodbye* with enormous pleasure. I read it straight through, with hardly a break, it is so damn readable! Unputdownable is not the right word, it's not a nail-biting thriller, it just flowed so easily and – apparently – effortlessly. It's sexy, funny, full of laconic and tender insights into the wonderful mess that people make of their relationships, and into that elusive prey we call love.'

Tim Pears

'Rogerson is a fine observer of human quirks, revealing a generous understanding of what it means to be an individual.'

Sunday Herald

'Rogerson's prose is impressive and deceptively powerful, making this a subtle and insightful read.'

The Big Issue

'Rogerson captures wonderfully the beauty and heartache of love and, as such, has chosen a theme we can all relate to.'

The Skinny

'A captivating and romantic novel following the lives of four characters and set in one of the most beautiful landscapes of Britain, the Scottish Highlands.'

lovereading.co.uk

'A charming tale of love and marriage . . . a wise sweet (bittersweet) book.'

Modern Scottish Collections (National Library of Scotland)

I Love You, Goodbye

I Love You, Goodbye

Cynthia Rogerson

BLACK & WHITE PUBLISHING

First published 2010
This edition published 2012
by Black & White Publishing Ltd
29 Ocean Drive, Edinburgh EH6 6JL

1 3 5 7 9 10 8 6 4 2   12 13 14 15

ISBN: 978 1 84502 435 2

A CIP catalogue record for this book is available
from the British Library.

Typeset by Ellipsis Digital Limited, Glasgow
Printed and bound by Nørhaven, Denmark

For the provost

Some species of limpets have homing instincts allowing them to return to the same spot on a rock. They leave a mucous trail behind them when they feed, which allows them to retrace their moves. This spot is known as a 'home scar' and the shape of a limpet's shell often grows to match the shape of its place on the rock.

Metro Factfile, Leith Walk bus

'Think you have some tiny idea of how love works? Are you high?'

Mark Morford, S.F. Chronicle

SEPTEMBER

Evanton

There is a small town in the Highlands of Scotland that from space looks like nothing, not even a dot. From Fyrish Hill, it looks like debris in a crevice, grey stone houses, snaking down towards the firth. Entering the town at twilight, it becomes the Shire. Cosily lit windows, with smoke curling from chimneys. Who wouldn't want to make their home here? But just a little bit closer, pressing up to these windows, things are not quite so idyllic. Of course not. And not only does every picturesque lane have the requisite unhappiness, every house does too. And every person.

Picturesque happiness being a hollow thing, Evantonians do not yearn for it. In any case, they are too busy to notice the absence of it. Look at them – there they are, living their lives, along with everyone else in the world. And in Inverness, which is two firths from Evanton, there is Ania, the Relate marriage counsellor, sitting in her apricot office at the top of the building. Very like a priest waiting in the dark of his confessional box.

Ania

What else matters, what else is truly interesting and mysterious, but love? Death, of course, but even that is hastened or hindered by love. And death of love is a uniquely human tragedy. There must be an evolutionary purpose for our grief at the end of love. I don't know what it is.

But the death of love brings me my livelihood, so I won't bemoan it too much. I have dipped into the intimate death throes of more than five hundred marriages now – a big tally for someone not yet thirty, but then I heard my calling early, and have devoted my life to resuscitating love. Marriage counselling is an art, and more. I am a doctor for terminally ill marriages. I station myself in the emergency room of relationships, and later, if I have failed, in the hospice. Above all, I am a philosopher of love.

You will be aware, if you are literary, that all happy families are alike, while all unhappy families are unhappy in their own way. I cannot add to this. People are lonely, they meet someone, they fall in love. They're better people, in love, and are quite easy to love back. In love, people are all the same. Love, during this phase, relies utterly on ignorance and unfamiliarity. As W. Somerset Maugham said, 'Love is what happens to a man and a woman who do not know each other.'

As for all my clients, by the time I meet them, often a quarter of a century into their marriages, it is different. You've no idea how fascinating it is, to observe daily how humans keep finding new ways to hurt each other. They *know* each other now. They have stopped trying; they have forgotten all their fears of loneliness and yearn for . . . a multitude of things that love has not, so far, yielded. Love has disappointed them, as it must.

I was born understanding this, but it didn't stop me marrying Ian. I hid my foreknowledge from him. What would be the point of spoiling his illusion? It would be like telling a two-year-old he will certainly die one day.

Love dies. There you go! It shouldn't surprise anyone, but it hits husbands and wives like cannon balls anyway. Most people think they've failed, as if breaking up wasn't inevitable. People whose love lasts a lifetime are aberrations. For the rest of us, even during the first kiss we taste the bittersweet end. And when we're honest, isn't heartbreak as exquisitely intense as the first flush of yearning? There are more poems and songs about falling out of love, than into love. The pain is certainly better than the dull plod of the middle phase. And when a relationship ends, well and truly, there's no more suspense about how it will end. There's anguish, but there is also a small amount of relief in knowing there can be no more. And then one can return to imagining that one will find someone even better.

If there were a government office called the Department of Human Love, a big pink room full of soft-bosomed women and cuddly dark-eyed men, they'd be inundated with complaints and questions every day. People would be suing Love for unimaginable damages.

But they can't, so they come to me.

I always have a moment, after they ring the doorbell, of closing my eyes and praying. Let me help these sore hearts, I ask no one in particular – the swirling atmosphere beyond the stars, the air in this room, the atoms of my own body. It calms me, asking for help. Then I open the door and let them in.

And there it is. There's the doorbell now.

Help me.

Rose

This is how I talk to my husband: 'So, get dressed! We're late for our Relate appointment. Your blue shirt's ironed. Not there, in the closet! Uhuh. And your shoes are needing replaced, look at the soles! Go on Monday to Clarks, they've a sale on.'

As if he's six years old. I can't remember when this started, this kind of patronizing impatience, this bossiness, but the momentum is powerful and now I can't stop even though I'd kill myself if I heard myself speak to me like this.

'I thought you said they had no appointments?' says Harry petulantly, as a six-year-old must, who wants to gain independence from his mother.

'God, do you never listen? I told you. They had a cancellation. We see Ania at eight o'clock.'

'Ania?'

'Yes, Ania.'

'Kind of like the sound of that. Foreign, but kind of soothing and wholesome. Classy. Polish?'

'How should I know? Shut up and get dressed.' Aren't I awful? I hate myself.

'A date with Ania. Yes! What should I wear? My blue shirt with those new black jeans? Those jeans aren't too naff are they?'

'Anything that's not your y-fronts. God you must be the last man in Britain to wear those. Amazing you can still buy them.'

'Do you not find them sexy then? I know these ones are kind of baggy and grey, but I could put on tighter newer ones, from Marks.'

'Right, as if that'd make a difference. Like anything would make a difference.'

'If you wore a nice thong from time to time, it might make a difference,' says my husband.

Pause, while I yank a brush through my hair and scowl. I am uglier and older tonight than usual. That is what my husband does to me. Uglifies me. A door closes down the hall, and I suddenly remember that I am also a terrible mother, as well as a terrible wife. He appears silently.

'Sam! Sam, dear, there's some dinner in the oven, I've left it on low. Just mind you switch it off after, right?'

'Where yous going?'

'Just out for a quick drink with friends. Won't be long, promise. Do you mind? You'll be alright, won't you? I'll leave my phone on.'

'Aye, course I'll be alright. Stay out all night if yous want.'

'Sam, don't be like that. Come back and give me a kiss. Sam!'

But he's gone back to his room, and there is my husband, standing in his y-fronts, with his white hairy belly protruding, saying: 'And I really do like that name. Ania.'

So we get in the car and head off. I spot couples everywhere, and none of them look like they're headed for a Relate date. They all look normal. They hold hands, and laugh. I bet they have songs that are their own songs. We never had a song. I don't know how, but we missed out on that stage. I wonder if marriages always happen in the same sequence, and whether it's too late now to get a song. I think it probably is. It's a lovely evening, but the loveliness is wasted on me. This grates too, this inability to enjoy the loveliness of the evening.

'Stop the car, I see it. But wait, do you think that's it? It says forty-seven on the door, it must be. But it looks just like a house.'

'Of course. They probably try not to draw attention to it,' says my sensible Harry, who has spent his life avoiding attention.

I feel strange, getting out of the car with Harry, who drives me insane, who drives me to infidelity and ugliness, but who is my familiar Harry. I catch his eye and a giggle begins to rise from my belly – there is cosiness to our own private hell. It contains many unpleasant emotions, but not uneasiness. But there's that momentum of antagonism again – habitual anger is a bitch to shift, even when it's not actually present. It seems to hold its shape even when it's empty.

'Ring the bell. Quick!' I bark, since he's reached the door first.

No noise at all, but there's a light on the top floor.

'You're blushing,' he points out.

'I'm embarrassed. It's the appropriate response to the situation. You would blush too if you were normal.'

'Yeah, like a normal man would've married you.'

'Fuck off,' I say automatically. 'And listen, we are not telling Ania about our sex life, right? Nothing about sex. I know what they're like . . . these therapist types. Feed on the intimate details of strangers' lives. No sex,' I hiss.

'Ok. No problem. No sex.'

'Ever.'

'No sex ever? You wish.'

And then the door opens. My heart is pounding, like it really is a date. I smile inappropriately, as if I'm falling in love.

'Good evening,' says an unlined young woman. I am fascinated by smooth skin these days. Her eyes shine, as if she knows us and is delighted.

'You must be Rose and Harry. I'm Ania, come in!'

Harry must be in love too, he has gone all pink and speechless.

Then he blurts out in his own inappropriate way: 'You have an unusual name, Ania.'

She turns and says: 'Yes. My father – he is Polish.'

Harry just stares – she is very pretty. In an anaemic way.

'Ania is a Polish name. Well, actually, it is a Polish way of saying Anka, another Polish name,' she says very slowly, like she's sussed already how slow Harry is. 'Which is my real name.'

'Polish!' he says, as if being Polish is like being from Mars.

'Yes, but I've always lived in Evanton. And my husband, he is from Evanton too,' she says almost defensively.

'We live in Evanton too! We've just moved there from Leith.'

'We're neighbours then,' she says coolly.

'Whereabouts in the village are you?'

Ania freezes for a second; there's probably some protocol where they use false names and never give out contact details, in case some estranged and deranged spouse seeks revenge.

'Harry! Don't be so nosey. Sorry, Ania.'

Ania pauses, then shakes her head once in a measured, assessing way. A woman of restraint and order. She'll hate me.

'Not far from you.'

'Amazing! And we never see each other! Isn't that just incredible?' says Harry.

'What an amazing coincidence!' I say.

We cannot stop ourselves; we are in competing gush mode. I feel self-loathing hover a millimetre away, the way it does at parties when I suddenly hear my own loud laugh and notice I am sloshing my fourth wine on the carpet, while dancing to music I hate. Abba.

'I think we probably do see each other all the time,' says Ania in a kind way, not at all my kind of irritated contradiction. 'We must. Evanton is so small. We see each other, but never notice.'

This is said with such calm certainty, and a kind of eerie professional indifference, we are both silenced, and follow this fair vision up two flights of stairs. Past closed office doors, past abstract watercolours, into an attic room painted apricot. Three gorgeous soft armchairs face each other. No furniture for more than one person. I choose a chair first, as if there's a race. I haven't been this nervous, or had this much fun with my husband, for years. Not since that time I thought his secretary fancied him.

'Now, make yourselves comfortable,' says Ania. Her voice is

warm and low and even. No accent, but there is something not quite Scottish about it. Or maybe her name has predisposed me to notice foreignness.

'My goodness, this is lovely. Such a comfy chair! And what a lovely colour on the walls!' I'm still gushing. I can't help it. I want Ania to like me. To be on my side.

'Thank you! I like people to feel at home here. Now, we have an hour, shall we get down to it?'

'Definitely,' says my husband in an uncharacteristically masterful way.

'Good. I believe in cutting straight to the root of the matter, so if you'd like to each tell me what you think the problem is, we can begin to fix it. What seems to be the main issue? You first, Harry. What makes you most unhappy about your marriage?'

'Our sex life,' says Harry.

Maciek

Please, I think about sex all the time. Of course! This doesn't stop me making good pizza. Funny – is same word at home, but here sounds very different. Less fuzzy. More . . . squeaky? Maybe it is only the way I hear. When customers come in, sometimes pizza is the only word I understand. They open their mouths and out comes noise, noise, noise, then this word. *Pizza.* It jumps out, and I say what I always say:

Mini? Medium? King?

If they haven't seen me here before, there's always a second of minute before they answer, and I know – I know what they are thinking. Who the fuck is this man, that he talks so strange? Some people, they give the piss because I speak this way. I sound stupid, like a three-year-old, when I speak with English. You can't know who I am in English, and I want, very much, for you to understand me. I am a serious person and I do not like to be laughed at.

Most customers in Pizza Palace are nice to me. They hear my strange speaking and they pause, not because they want to hate foreigners, but because they're curious. I can see it; it's in their eyes. Most are too shy to ask where I am from, or what I am doing, popping up in their high street Pizza Palace shop.

They pause, then answer:

Pepperoni, king size.

Pizza can be a world. There are so many steps to making pizza. First you must chop and grate and slice all the things that go on top, and then put them into their own little metal trays. You think this can't be a world, but you've never tried, perhaps. You have no need to make worlds of silly things like pizza. I understand.

But I need to feel good, or it all goes wrong. My customer, he doesn't like it and complains to his friends, and they don't come again. Scottish people, they're strange that way. They love to complain. Complain, complain, complain! But not to someone who can fix things because then it might get fixed and they'd have nothing to complain about. I've been here four months, and I've learned much.

Ok, here is a couple. Look at them, making me jealous with their couple-ness. They look fed up. He doesn't hold the door open for her, and she doesn't talk to him. I can tell this about them right away: They will order two pizzas, not one large one.

'Hurry up Harry, for God's sake, I'm starving.'

'Yeah, all that sex talk gives me an appetite too.'

I like this man. He says sex like he is saying . . . hamburger. Or welly boot. He brings back the laugh feeling.

'Good evening,' says this woman who must be his wife, because she has not looked at him.

'Yes? Please, I can help you?' I say, very polite, and of course, in the English that makes me sound like a different person, a much stupider man. But you know different already, right?

'I'll have a margarita mini, please. Well, come on Harry, the poor man's waiting!'

'Hold on, I'm still thinking. Could you make a king-size meat feast with mushrooms?'

'Yes, I can do this things.' And I begin. Lay the bases out, brush them with sauce.

'Nice hat,' says this man I already like. I know it is a nice hat, because people are always telling me this. I wear it all the time. It is very old, but still has a good shape. Men used to wear hats like this every day. I don't know why they don't anymore.

'Where are you from?'

'I am from Krakow. This is in Poland.' I give my best smile, not too much smile. The one I use to get this job.

'Are you? How fascinating. We met someone else Polish tonight. Do you like it here? Do you not miss your home?'

I could tell him about my caravan at Evanton, the way it smells, always, of gas and damp, and the stain with fur that lives near the toilet and the way Mr McKenzie, he bangs on my door Fridays for rent. Never with a smile, and it always hurts that he doesn't like me. Stupid I know. To care about Mr McKenzie.

And home . . . I could tell this man about the *pierogi* – perfect parcels of gorgeous pasta – and cherry tea in glass mugs, and the way there is only standing room in Bazylika Mariacka at Sunday Mass, and the boys who always break-dance in the cobblestones of the square, with just a piece of old cardboard under their heads. And the food on the shelves in Pawelek's shop, the shiny herrings in jars. And my office at the college. That huge window, the pigeons that crowd up on the ledge.

I could even tell him about Marja, and the way one day, I find the street is not big enough. Then Krakow is not big enough, and yes – soon all of Poland, it is too small. Too near her. So I leave. Some Poles, most Poles, come to Britain for better money. I come because Marja, she stops loving me.

'Yes, some days I miss home a little bit,' I tell him. 'But I like Scotland. Here is fine.'

Then I focus on the pizza because this pizza, it is where I am right now.

Sam

I know why we're here. I was there, for fuck's sake. I had that slow death. My parents are totally gay.

See, living in Evanton's pure stupid. And it sucks every minute. They never even asked me did I want to move from Leith, they just like do whatever they want and drag me along.

Hey, I'm a freak here. And I feel sick every day when I wake up.

But today I meet someone who's not a total twat. He's not from here either. He makes the pizzas in the shop that's so wee it only has him in it. Kyle and his pals are at their usual game at lunchtime, and he lets me stay in the shop till they clear off.

'You don't go back to school now?' he asks.

'Nah,' I told him. 'School's shite.'

Then he says: 'You don't eat lunch? You don't want pizza?'

'Can I have just one slice?'

'One slice? Not a mini pizza?'

'I've only seventy-five pence.'

'Ah.'

'Oh, that's ok, I'm not really hungry.' And when I hear myself say this, my throat suddenly hurts, and my voice cracks up a bit. As if I didn't feel bad enough already. I hate it when I can hear myself talk and my voice starts wibbling around. I'm fucking starving.

Then he asks: 'What your name is, please?'

He speaks good, but gets his words in a funny order.

'Sam,' I tell him, though I'm feeling so boab, even my name sounds stupid to me.

He tells me his name and we shake hands over the counter. His hand is huge, and I mean fucking massive. Then he says this cool thing:

'You want small job, Sam, then I give you pizza for no money?'

Totally pervy thing to say, I know, but he's so not.

'Aye, thanks a lot.'

So I ask him his name again, to be polite, and I say it wrong at least six times. But I work at it, and now his name's ok. I just think: Magic. Magic, with a French accent. Majeek.

He gives me the brush and points to floor.

'Aye, right. I can sweep, no bother.'

'Pepperoni?'

'Aye, pepperoni's sound. Hey, you're Polish, right?' Cause I am suddenly wondering if he just has a speech defect.

'Yes.'

'Thought so. Sound.'

Then we just stop talking and work.

This is the best thing to happen to me since we came to this hell hole. Maciek's legend. And he speaks my language! Hardly at all.

Ania

As a rule, we hardly ever talk at breakfast, unless we have something important to say. For instance:

'I'll be late home tonight, it's parents' night,' says Ian, and yawns, as if nothing is different.

As if he had not asked me for a baby last night. Whispered it actually. Yet here he is this morning, eating his bran flakes and reading yesterday's *Independent*, his face the usual face – a bit distant and bland and slightly amused. No clue on it, of last night's whispered wants, his eyes fixed on mine. And nothing unusual in the day leading up to the whisper. A typical Sunday.

I am a firm believer in lists. We ticked off things on our to-do list; he cut the lawn for the last time this year, I painted the bathroom windowsill where it gets mouldy. Tick, tick. We ticked things off our to-buy list; food, cushion covers, daffodil bulbs. Tick, tick, tick. We ate dinner (beef and tomato casserole), drank wine (Rioja, £7.99), watched a politically aware DVD (*Shooting Dogs*). Went to bed and had our usual Sunday night's love-making.

It was, as usual, nice. I paced myself, concentrated and made sure I came, let him know when he could come, which he did. I didn't look at his face when he came, but I imagine he had his eyes closed and looked in pain. I make a point of never letting a week go by without a lengthy session under the duvet, and somehow this has drifted into a Sunday night ritual – as if we procrastinate doing it all week, till Sunday is the only day left to do it, the last item on the to-do list. Our hot date.

Married sex is like a body balance class. How many women actually want to go to a body balance class? Aside from the two who have all the gear and always show up early. But women always have a glow after, and can look forward to six days before the next class. All the studies suggest that regular intercourse, not just cuddles, not even just oral sex or masturbation, but out and out sex is required to lower chances of certain kinds of cancer. Like red wine, sex lowers blood pressure. I advise all my sex-weary clients to go through the motions. Sometimes the real thing will be tricked by the façade and sneak in, and it will not be a chore. If it does not sneak in, at least you will have lowered risks of cervical cancer and heart disease. Like art, it should not need to wait for a muse to begin. It is the process of doing it, of painting or writing or composing, which creates the magic that makes art possible. Making love can create love, where there was only indifference before. Where there was only coldness and sadness and distance. You don't believe me? Try it.

Now Rose and Harry, my newest clients, are a classic example of a couple who have gotten out of the habit of sex. Rose finds it difficult to feel attracted to Harry again. She has forgotten how it goes. I explained to her: Libidos are like muscles. If you don't exercise at all, you will find it not only impossible, but undesirable, to climb a mountain. Or even ride a bike to the shops. Love has rules, and the rules must be respected. I try not to lecture, but it is difficult. Rose and Harry are so naïve. They actually believe things like thongs and flings are the issues. But then all my clients seem like love-laymen to me.

You know what I want to tell Rose and Harry? Love exists outside ourselves. It is impersonal and available to anyone who understands how to tap into it. The choice is not who to love, or how to love, but simply to love or not. Yes, the scariest truth about love is that it is random. Why do you think I married so young? I didn't see much point in wasting years searching for the most compatible man. I looked around me for a good man, a kind man, and the world is heaving with these. It is, really it is. Physically beautiful people with charm and talent may be thin on the ground, but good people are everywhere. Ian was good, he was kind, but he did not make my heart race. I chose him, poured love into him; I grew my lover.

So last night, there we were, in the dark, mutually sated, and just as I am drifting off, spooned into my husband's lap, he reaches out and strokes my face. This irritates me at first. I have just begun my descent into sleep, a very delicious sleep. The sleep of the righteous you might say, but then I am not righteous, just being who I am. Anyway, he strokes my face, as if he is blind and reading Braille. There is so much in those fingers I have to turn to him.

'What,' I say, not ask.

'Ania?' whispered like a sigh.

'Aye?' I can feel sleep receding further. Like an ebbing wave of oblivion. Please shut up, I will my husband. But I never say shut up to Ian out loud. I understand how corrosive it is in a marriage to speak with disrespect. Another rule.

'Ania, do you think it's time we started a family?'

'A baby?'

'Aye, a baby. Do you not fancy a baby?'

I instinctively swoop my hand down to my belly, my smooth flat belly that I am very proud of. I never overeat and I swim every Tuesday. I deserve this belly.

'Ania? I do love you, Ania,' he whispers, as if disputing something I have said.

'Come on. I *love* you!' he says again.

Ian rarely says I love you. This is more alarming than the baby request. Of course, I tell him that I love him quite often, when I say goodnight, or he gives me a present for my birthday. I tell him I love him, and then I tell him: And you love me! We love each other! I understand how important it is to say. Like sex, I-love-you should be said regularly or it gets dried up and lost.

Honesty is overrated; I say it with no feeling at all sometimes, because wives should tell their husbands they love them. It makes husbands feel secure, and secure husbands make more loving husbands, which can actually make saying I love you the next time a more natural outpouring. This is something else I tell my clients. A love trick. Lying.

I could see Rose liked this idea of lying, though Harry flinched like a betrayed spouse, which I guess he is. It gets dressed up in lots of names, but sexual jealousy is usually what brings them here. I tried to explain to them that after a certain period, love in a marriage is not natural. Not spontaneous. It is a job that must be attended to every single day, a fragile plant that must be watered just so much and no more. A goldfish that must neither be neglected nor overfed, like the goldfish in *A Fish Out of Water* that ends up outgrowing a swimming pool.

Odd that when Ian finally does say I love you, unprompted, I find I cannot say it back. Very odd. I put it on my to-think-about list for tomorrow. Why I cannot say it now. But I do love Ian. *I do.* For a full minute I look out the window at the moon and the dark outline of Fyrish. Then I turn and say:

'Good, Ian. Thank you.'

I say this as if his tenderness is merely good manners.

Then I hear myself say, because I also have good manners, and because I know it would be good for us, and appropriate, given the spare room, our ages, our health, our whole life:

'Yes, I do want a baby Ian. We'll have a baby, will we? Yes.'

Then we begin to make love again, this time without a condom.

And here we are, eating breakfast as if our old life wasn't now over. As if the molecules of a new being might not be spinning already. 'Pass the milk, darling,' I say, and he does, in his usual way.

Rose

Some parts of our old life have continued. I'm still a cook, though being a school dinner lady is a bit of a comedown after cheffing at Kingfishers. Never planned on cooking being a long-term thing; funny how life works out, eh? I mean, my folks had plans for me to go to uni – they've both got degrees – but I never even liked school. Loved reading; still do. Just couldn't hack the whole exam thing. Classic under-achiever, they called me, as if that was a bad thing. As if having a professional career was the only road to the good life. Fuck school. But the weird thing is, here I am, going to school again every morning. Can't see myself sticking with it forever, but it's not a bad job, not really. I like the way it doesn't use up my brain. I tell myself stories. Sing songs in my head. Listen and watch stuff. Money's pretty crap compared to Kingfishers, but you can't beat the hours of a school job.

Oh, who am I kidding? I hate my job. I'm bored out of my head, most of the time. It feels like decades ago I made some fundamental mistakes out of sheer carelessness, and now I'm stuck, well and truly, in the wrong life. I should have gone to university, got a degree, found some interesting career. Shouldn't have married Harry. Mum and Dad were right. The older I get, the more obvious it is. I've screwed up.

I bet you thought dinner ladies are always sweet dears who go home to knit and bake scones. Some are darlings, wholesome scone bakers, but some are like me. I have to cover shifts sometimes for dinner ladies with hangovers, or depression. Or for Lily, my new pal here who, when her oil worker hubby finally comes home, is too shagged out to come to work.

But listen, dinner ladies deserve a lot of respect. They get to see more than you think, and no one even notices them. I've only been working this job a month, and I already know which kids don't get breakfast at home, which kids have no friends, and which kids are so competitive they think even eating is a race. And the things you overhear! Yesterday, one little girl asking her pal, tactfully, if her parents were un-divorced, as if having married parents was just pure embarrassing.

The kids I really feel sorry for are the loners. You can tell by the way they sit and eat, all hunched up, jamming the food in, and usually too much food. Other kids think they have a disease or something. No one wants to sit with them, because no one is sitting with them. And they look miserable, no matter how basically good-looking they are. Other kids – the same ones, every day – are always getting their crisps grabbed and stood on, or their milk spilled, by twisted mean kids – and these mean kids have their own reasons for being miserable and needing to bully. I tell you, dinner ladies totally understand that being a kid is *hell* for some kids. It is brutal in the lunchroom, and even worse in the playground after lunch. I used to watch Sam. I'd wander by the school at lunchtime, spy on him. He always had a nice group of pals, I was glad to see.

Like all jobs, we have our routines, but every day is different – Monday's pizza, Tuesday's lasagne, Wednesday's sausages, Thursday's fish, Friday's mince and tatties. Other stuff too, but those are the main meals. So each day is flavoured by the food. I always think of good days as mince and tattie days. The kids clean their plates, and it's easy to cook. Bad days are lasagne days, with fancy salads and four steps to making the lasagne. All the waste, kids pretending to be allergic to tomatoes, and the whole school seems cranky after.

Today is a lasagne day, dinner lady code for a crap day. It's Sam's parents' night, and here I am. Christ. This could be my old school, back in Morningside. The same graffitied walls, same stink of cheap deodorant. The same depressing echoing sensation. Why do secondary schools have to be so dire, when primaries mostly manage to be sweet and wholesome? Kiltearn Primary, where I work, has a much more innocent stink. It smells of talcum powder and pee and disinfectant, and the walls are plastered with butterflies and rainbows. No swears anywhere.

Here, there are photographs of the entire school when it was small enough to have all the pupils in one photo. And plaques with the names of former pupils who died as soldiers, not long after leaving school. Waiting our turn to see Sam's English teacher, I say their names aloud in my head, to make myself believe they belonged to real boys who bled to death on French beaches and fields. It works, and my throat aches for Ian MacKay and Murdo MacKenzie. *They existed.* I'm morbid. Some people think morbid's a bad thing. But I think feeling sad about young men dying is better than . . . worrying about what soap powder gets wine stains out best. Anyway, if they're not supposed to be thought about, remembered, then what's the point of their names on a plaque?

Harry's looking at nothing, at the air in front of his eyes. Face all slack, quite dim looking. Probably thinking about some new short skirt Angela in the office had on today. He works as an estate agent, just like in Leith – in fact, it's the same company, that's how we came to be here – he asked for a transfer, and Dingwall was the first vacancy that came up. God bless Your Move. Sorted the whole thing out in a day. I've seen Angela and her skirts, the way they ride up her thighs when she sits. What a hypocrite he is, all the things he accuses me of. As if he wouldn't too, if Angela gave him the look. I don't understand Harry, but god help me, I know that man. I know exactly how many seconds he'd hesitate before screwing around.

Our turn at last. Mr MacLeod, the English teacher, is about thirty. Bit girly, narrow shoulders, sweet face.

'Sam? Ah yes, Sam!' he says, running his finger down a printed sheet as if it's littered with children. Bet he doesn't even remember Sam. Teachers still irritate me, to tell the truth. And scare me.

'Sam is, well, he's a reluctant reader, at least with the texts we're using, but he is certainly a good writer. Messy handwriting, of course, but it's obvious Sam's a bright boy. However, there is the behaviour problem. I've had to move him away from his friends. They seem to distract him a lot.'

'His friends? He has friends? What are their names?'

'Rose, stop it, that's hardly our business.'

'Well, but I am so relieved. I often worry he's lonely, being an only child and a new kid here. He spends a lot of time alone in his room.'

'Why not ask your son about them?'

'I will,' I say.

'We will not,' asserts Harry. 'Leave the poor boy be.'

'Anyway,' says Mr MacLeod. 'Sam is, shall we say, taking his time with the books we're reading at present. Does he read much at home?'

'Well,' I begin. 'I bought him the books about the series of weird bad stuff. And I read to him a lot, when he was wee.'

'Read?' scoffs Harry. 'Nah, not likely! Sam's always on the computer, or watching telly. Can't say I've seen him actually reading. Ever. Why, do you think he should read? Never been a reader myself,' says Harry proudly. 'Can't see the point of novels. Rose, now she reads all the time. More of a girl thing, reading, isn't it?'

There is a pause, while I make a mental note to not tell Harry about the next parents' night. Or the one after that. Mr MacLeod smiles politely at Harry.

'Sam has reading homework most nights. It might help matters if you were to remind him of this homework, and perhaps have a look at it yourselves. Or set aside time when the television and computer are off bounds, so there is less distraction, or temptation.'

'Yes, quite right,' I say.

'Excellent,' he says. 'Well, it was nice to meet you both. And please don't forget about Sam's homework!'

'MacLeod,' muses Harry as we walk to the car. 'Wonder if he's related to our Ania MacLeod?'

'Doubt it,' I say. 'Millions of MacLeods here.'

Bet he's obsessing about Ania now. Got her down to a thong.

Back home, over tea, Harry reminds me we have homework too. Ania has given me instructions to have sex with my husband. Homework! Punishment, more like. Like eating the cold dried-up peas on my plate because I had to clean it. Forced eating – doesn't that result in eating disorders? I still hate peas, and have never forced Sam to eat anything. Mind you, it's a miracle that boy is alive. I have no idea what he eats. Sam seems to hate anything I touch. In fact, it is pretty obvious that Sam hates me now. I don't get it. When did that happen?

And I hate Harry. Look at him, eating with his mouth open, just shovelling it in like a pig. I used to try to get him to eat with his mouth shut. Back when I imagined I could change anything about him. That he'd want to change, simply to please me. If he gets to eat like that, then I get to refuse him sex.

'Right then, wife of mine,' Harry says, swallowing the last of his chips at the same time. 'Tonight's the night, eh?'

Then he leers at me. Leers! A self-mocking leer, but a leer nonetheless. At his wife of twenty-two years. Twenty-four years, if you count the two years of shagging that led to marriage. Oh aye, I used to really fancy that kind of thing with Harry. Before I really knew him. I used to look at him and not feel the earth under my feet. Harry was hot. Now he's not even lukewarm. Inside his mouth is kind of slimy, and his moves haven't changed since he first got laid. But to be honest, those aren't the main reasons I've gone off him. Alpin's not exactly a hunk or a super-lover, but I could lick every part of him all day long. I'm off Harry because he pisses me off so much. I can't imagine Alpin ever pissing me off. We are perfect together.

'Oh fuck off, Harry.'

'What a come on! Teasing the old man like that. Well, I know just the answer to cheeky, naughty wives. Come on, over the kitchen table!' This is like the leer – a self-mocking tone. Harry knows he sounds naff, but it's like they're the only words he knows. I actually feel sorry for the man. In between despising him.

'Just the answer,' I sneer. He leers and I sneer. It's eerie.

'That's right. Got it right here, you lucky girl.'

'Would that, by any chance, be the same answer you have for . . . *every fucking thing*?'

'Now, there's no denying it works.'

'I deny it. Again.'

I give him my piss-off-and-die look. He doesn't flinch, but turns and leaves the room, and there's something in his shoulders and back, especially the back of his neck. My arrows have found a home.

Oh shit! Some days I feel like I've spent decades being angry, trying to defeat this man's ego, to emasculate him, and yet the second I succeed I'm filled with self-loathing. Hello self-loathing, my old friend; I've come to talk to you again. But when he comes back through, jacket on, and announces in a brusque voice: 'I'm out for a pint,' I don't even look at him. Just wave my hand in his direction. Like I'm shooing off some pesky fly.

I pour a glass of red wine and run a bath in what I still think of as the new bathroom. Like I still think of this house as the new house, and this life in Evanton as my new life. All the new things that were supposed to fix me. Well, they *are* all new, and no, of course they *are not* fixing me. Fuck off. As if it was that simple.

It wasn't just Alpin's kiss, you know. It sounds strange, but I'd become almost viscerally aware of the passing of time, especially when taking the rubbish out or washing dishes. My heart – it'd race doing these things, as if time was a substance literally running through my flesh. I can't be here again at the sink, already! I'd think. Where did the entire day go? At this rate I'll be dead by tomorrow. And all along, for years and years, I'd had this waiting sensation. Life was fine, but every day I woke up full of expectancy, and I didn't even know what I was waiting for. But I knew, most definitely knew in a sickening way, that it had not arrived, and that Harry was no part of it.

How could he be? Harry is anti-life.

Always wants to leave parties early, hates dancing, hates books, hates art, hates travelling, hates my parents, hates to spend money on clothes, hates to spend money on anything. And the worse thing of all: Harry has never been the slightest bit curious about me. He's anti-me! I might say I spent all day in bed, and he'd never ask why. Or I might say I just finished reading an amazing novel; he'd never ask what it's about, or if he can read it. I could look like hell, or look like a fucking beauty queen – Harry would just ask: When's tea ready?

He defends himself by saying it's not fair to accuse of him of not being someone else, as if I hadn't known who he was when we married. He's not a reader, never has been. He isn't psychic, how would he know I'd been sick? And actually, he just doesn't like foreign food that much, and was that a crime?

Basically this is what our fights boil down to:

Me: 'Can we please do blahblahblah for a change?'

Harry: 'No.'

Me: 'But you know it would make me happy. Isn't that a good enough reason? We always do just what you want.'

Harry: 'That is just not true. Stop being so spoiled. Stop being so ungrateful.'

Me: 'So we can't do blahblahblah?'

Harry: Silence. Probably putting kettle on.

Me: 'You're such a smug fuckfaced selfish fucking arsehole. You never think about anyone but yourself.' Sputtering. Red faced and hating the way I sound.

Harry: 'Stop exaggerating,' said quietly. 'You always have to exaggerate.'

And then we don't talk for a while. No make-up scene. No resolution. Then in a few hours, or days, we start acting normal again, till the next fight. Which is the same as the last. Round and round.

Kissing Alpin changed everything. He kissed me as we were leaving his and Sarah's house one evening, after a dinner party, and we somehow caught each other's lips instead of cheeks. An accidental kiss. Harry was ahead of me, in the car already. Alpin kissed me on my lips, and somehow even though it was supposed to be a casual social kiss, we let it linger for a few seconds. Maybe just three. All the way home in the dark car, I felt this kiss on my mouth, growing, till it spread right down through to my toes. I had a little crush on Alpin already of course; he was endless fun to talk to. He'd read all the novels I liked, had all the CDs I liked. Loved to walk, dance, get pissed. Effortless rapport. And now, this. This kiss, which felt like it should be in capital letters. THE KISS. I pretended to nap in the car, so I could savour it.

We met in secret. We met whenever we could. I was in love, and so was he. We told each other so all the time. We met when we were supposed to be at work, or on some errand. We made love in each other's marital beds, and didn't feel guilty at all. It was intoxicating, addicting. I told myself nothing else mattered. I couldn't be without him. It felt so good to love someone at last, with no holds barred. Like an outpouring, from a place that never emptied. My heart, I suppose. The valves were jammed on whenever I was with Alpin. At home, they shut down, allowing the minimum necessary blood flow through. Never that generous feeling, that openness. I began to really despise the mean, angry self I always was with Harry.

And then we became a cliché. Harry found out in the usual way. My x-rated emails. And we had the usual marital crisis, the one that's enacted in millions of homes like ours, all over the country, every day. With both of us losing weight and sleep, him suddenly noticing me – what I wore, where I went, who I saw. Demanding all the details. I lied, of course. Told Harry it had only been the once, and it was over, and not that great anyway. A moment of inebriated lust. Wasn't sure what I was going to do, and didn't want to burn bridges yet.

Jealousy finally woke Harry up to me, but too late. Our marriage was hell before, only he didn't know it – now it was hell for us both. Constantly panicky, both of us weeping and accusing each other. Never told Sam. Figured it would just screw him up, and God knows if you are fourteen, you are already pretty screwed for a few years. We fought and wept and hissed and tore our hair out, mostly in the privacy of our bedroom, or on long walks by the canal.

And in the end, I renounced my lover, my true love. Gave Alpin up, like tobacco, and became good again! This felt instantly flat and depressing, but the prospect of divorce was too scary. Anyway – who would I be leaving Harry for? Alpin was in love with me, but he loved his lovely wife Sarah. And his children. And his millions of in-laws. They all went on holiday together every year, to places like Keffalonia. It was hopeless. I told Alpin goodbye, secretly hoping he'd object violently, sweep me off into the sunset. But he seemed relieved.

'Best this way, I suppose,' he said sadly.

'Aye. Too much at stake.'

'It's the kids.'

'Aye. The kids.'

'Anyway, I'd drive you crazy, if I lived with you.'

'We'd drive each other crazy.'

Sarah never knew, and we all pretended it never happened. And though he never actually came out and admitted it, Harry deciding to take this Dingwall job a few months later was definitely down to Alpin. Harry asked me to never mention Alpin again, in that context, and after a while, because no one else knew, it all started to seem surreal. As if I had just imagined it all. I ached to ring Alpin, to talk to him, tell him how much I missed him. Hold him. But I didn't, and he didn't try to contact me either. Alpin and Sarah came to our farewell open house, and he actually shook Harry's hand. His smile seemed genuinely warm and uncomplicated. This hurt more than anything. His happiness made a fool of me.

Now, 200 miles and thirteen months from that first kiss, I light a candle, try to feel at home in my new bathroom. Relax into the bubbles. Rose scented. The Mark Knopfler and Emmylou Harris CD I put on earlier drifts through the door. Nothing like a bit of toned-down country. I admire my own flesh, which in the candlelight and bubbles, and without my glasses, isn't too bad. Harry's wrong, and so is that sanctimonious Ania woman. Great word, sanctimonious. Nothing wrong with me. I'm not frigid, I'm the opposite. I can't bear to be touched by a man I don't fancy. It is an anathema to me. Oh god, another great word, and I finally found a way to use it.

'Anathema!' I say out loud.

I read constantly, so my head is full to bursting with words I've never heard aloud, much less said. There they sit in my brain, waiting for their time, while I chop onions and fry mince for eighty. Love it when they find their way to my tongue.

Poor me. God knows I wish it wasn't true, but I am very, very, very, very tired of not fancying Harry. I am old with not wanting him. It is eroding away my life. Melodrama cannot begin to describe how even my breathing is affected. And it feels like a waste of life. Such a waste of capacity for passion. Before Alpin I was a happily discontented wife. Now I am an unhappily discontented wife, who thinks about her ex-lover too often, who talks to her husband mostly through a Polish-Scottish woman called Ania, and who forgets to feed her thirteen-year-old son balanced meals.

Shit – Sam! Did I see him when we came in? I'm pretty sure I heard some telly noise from his bedroom, but did I actually see him? What is happening to my maternal instincts? Menopause has produced a kind of static in the air around me, and I can't receive signals with the normal clarity.

'Check Sam when out of bath,' I order myself out loud. 'Ask

him what he's reading in English class. Try to kiss him. Yeah, that'll be right.'

Then I lie there in the bath thinking how my voice sounds. Middle-aged and a little demented.

'Shit shit shit.'

Consider shaving my legs; decide not to. Who for? I rub lotion into my skin after I'm dry, and pay special attention to my face, chin up. I don't look at the mirror; that way lies madness. Leave the bathroom, wrapped in my towel, just as Harry walks back into the house.

'Rose? I'm back!'

He always shouts this when he comes home. There's no hurt in his voice now, he's returned an undefeated, inebriated man. His heavy feet march into the hall, where I, still slightly greasy, stand.

'Ah! Aha!' he says, eyeing my bare limbs.

'Did you close the door properly?' I snap. 'I can feel a draught.'

'Of course I did. You're cold? Come here, I'll warm you.'

I pull the towel closer and hurry past him, hugging the wall.

'Put the kettle on, will you Harry?' To soften my mean hurrying and wall-hugging.

I own sexy nightgowns and underwear. People give them to me for presents; Alpin gave me a pair of French knickers, and Harry's given me some too. Look, there they are, in my top drawer. Now and then I almost give them away, or toss them, but then I think: Who knows who I will become one day? I may want them.

But tonight the sight of them depresses me. What if I never want to encourage any man again? What if from now on I am a frozen woman, a do-not-touch-me woman till I die? What if I never kiss anyone but Harry for the rest of my life? I can't forget the way it felt with Alpin. How I could not imagine getting to the end of wanting him. Of kissing him. It was like Pandora's Box. Now I'd been reminded of how it could be, how could I ever settle for anything less?

This marriage has to end or I will die.

Quickly followed by the equally familiar:

If this marriage ends, I will die.

Better Harry than the spectre of loneliness.

'Kettle's boiled!' shouts Harry, in his usual robust way. Relieved that again I've not squashed him, I hurry to the kitchen, clad from head to toe in my ancient robe.

'So,' says my husband, handing me a cup of tea. He eyes my bundled up body, and tsks and sighs. 'Oh dear. What will Ania say? What *will* she say?'

'Oh fuck off Harry. I'll tell her I'm allergic to sex. Or just tell her you piss me off too much for me to fancy you. Suck it up, ok?'

'God I love it when you talk dirty.'

I smile, but not outwardly. One of the ways I punish him for failing to attract me is that I never let Harry see how he amuses me. Harry is an arsehole, but I am a truly terrible wife. And my god! I've forgotten to check Sam again.

And much later, when I am fully awake and it's 3:20 again, my heart hammers at the sheer number of possible tragedies lying in wait. And all the times I have been rejected, all the times I have screwed up, pop up to say hello.

Arsehole or not, I'm glad Harry's here. Breathing next to me.

Hell. Love is irrelevant at 3:20 in the morning.

Maciek

3:20. Almost six hours to go.

No sex for five weeks now. I am not going to think about this.

A medium red-hot pepper pizza, with extra cheese.

Three mini ham and pineapple pizzas, one with mushrooms and garlic.

Anyway, what is sex? It is nothing. Sex! It leads to trouble. Women, after sex they all want love. I've been in love; love can kill a man. I don't want love, I just want sex.

A king-sized margarita for this woman with her four little children, noses with snot running, each of them, and she dries the noses with an old nappy and gives the baby a tickling till he laughs.

'Mum!' whine the older ones, jealous. 'Me too!'

Of course, I had a Mama, my Mamusia, and she tickled me too. She dies a long time ago. Before I am six. My father? No one speaks to me of this man. I never meet him.

Am I sad about these things? No. I was not very sad then either. I am too busy being a kid, I guess.

This is what I remember: Night time, Mamusia getting into my bed and telling me stories till I tumble into sleep. She never leaves till I am asleep. Sometimes I close my eyes, like this, and make my breathing like sleeping breathing. That's how I know that always, even when I am asleep, she kisses me before she leaves my room. On my forehead, right here.

She has a dress with red roses. And a necklace with small yellow balls. Pearls? She always let me play with this and one day it breaks and the pearls roll everywhere. Mamusia, at first she looks very angry. Her hand wants to slap me. Maybe I look funny, because then she laughs. Laughs and laughs. I remember that slap that never lands on me. My skin tingles there. And I laugh too, the kind of laugh that is like a wriggle in your stomach. Till you laugh without noise. Her name is Wisia. A little bit hard, that name. She is softer than her name.

On the last morning, she walks me to my school. It is a day like all the other days. Same time, same rush because we are late, always. And rain! I wear my yellow rain jacket, and she holds the umbrella over me. Not over herself. I know this, because I can still see her wet hair. The way it sticks to her neck.

The medium red-hot peppers pizza is ready. I slide it out, slide the minis in. Slice the red-hot one, ready for the box.

But I can't remember what Mamusia says on that last morning because I don't listen. Of course. I don't know it is the last time. How can I? It is a morning like all mornings. Rain, school, rush. She probably kisses me and says: Be a good boy, my Macius, which is what only she calls me. Never Maciek.

Be my good boy, Macius.

After school my aunt, Ciotka Agata, she meets me, and she has a bag with my pyjamas in it. Maybe I ask where Mamusia is and she explains. I don't remember that part. We go to her house, and she shows me my new room. A nice, big room. People give me things, a train that winds up and makes a whistle noise. I'm happy because I have new toys. One day I remember to be sad, but everyone else, they are not crying anymore. And no one talks about her. Soon, I lose her face. Just parts of her stay. The rose dress. Her wet hair. The goodnight kiss. There is a photograph Ciotka Agata, she keeps on the mantlepiece. I steal this photograph one day, keep it in my bedroom, inside a book. And now it's in my caravan. In this photograph, Mamusia is about sixteen. She doesn't know about me. There is a smile in her eyes and her mouth is open, like she is speaking. She is not beautiful. I can see this. A bit fat, I think. A nose that is too big. In this photograph, she's looking right at the camera. At the photographer. I pretend it's me. And I make up the words she's saying. If I say my name the way she used to say it, out loud, *Macius*, it makes me feel light.

When I was seventeen, I give my virginity to a dark-eyed girl whose perfume reminds me of Mamusia. Evening in Paris. This is easy to steal, and I have this bottle still. It's in the drawer under her photograph.

Out with the minis, and finally in with the king-sized margarita. The mother waits outside now, and her kids run in the little circles she allows them to play in. Sometime there are cars on the high street, though it is a pedestrian high street. She looks out for cars.

I think about her more now. If that's what missing someone is, then I miss Mamusia.

I meet lots of girls, lots of girlfriends. There is Alicja who smells of roses, and Karolina with the red hair. And Stefania, whose mother always kisses me on the lips. There is always a woman's hand to hold, in those days. And with each woman, at the beginning, I always tell myself: This one, I will marry. I am a very serious man, I already tell you this. But something, it always happens, and I stop thinking we will marry. Always, this happens before six months. I end it. Me! No girl ends it, always it is Maciek who says *pozegnalny*. After ten or twelve years, I stop being surprised; I just wait for this ending time to come. I hate this time of not thinking a woman is beautiful anymore.

Two years ago, just before I am thirty-five, I fall in love with Marja. The woman who moves into the flat downstairs, and who gives me huge smile the first time we meet on the landing. I am happy! As simple and miraculous as her smile. The day after we meet, she is in my bed. No time to think, to change sheets, to analyse, to wonder if we are in love. We live together for a year, and always, it has a feeling of rightness to it. Never live with a woman before, but no matter. She does not ask and I do not tell her, for me this is new. Did I ever look at her and think: Who is this woman, and what is she doing in my flat? No. I don't remember thinking about us at all, which is strange because I spent my days thinking about the meaning of life. Explaining things like Positivism, and thoughts of men long dead, to classrooms of students. I work at the college, then. Not the university – I am not that good. I teach philosophy. I talk about how post-war Europe grows to suspect romanticism, idealism. I give lectures about Julian Ochorowicz and Jan Lukasiewicz, Kant and Schopenhauer. I explain what they all think about God. About life after death. What is right way and what is wrong way to live. What is important and what is . . . pepperoni. Phenomenology, it is my favourite. No wonder Karol Wojtyla, he becomes Pope. He likes phenomenology too much.

Philosophy, it is vodka bottles with lots of pretty labels, telling you about the best vodka inside. I know this! I watch my students, they lurch from one philosopher to another, like drunks, like wanton women always loving best the man they are with.

It made my head hurt some days, to tell the truth. But with Marja, life is easy. Relaxing. It is her tossing a bunch of ingredients, slap dash, into a big steaming pot, all the while telling me her day, and laughing often. Or singing. Marja, she sings all the time. Terrible voice – off key and too high. Screechy! She sings on the stairs coming home, so I hear her even before her key is in the door. I never ask myself: Maciek! What will you do if this ends?

The king-sized is now almost ready. I take more orders. Medium meat feast, one mini anchovy. I re-fill cheese tub and onions tub. And fold open more boxes, ready for pizzas. They are warm and dry because I keep them on top of the oven.

Just before I lose my job at the college – yes, bad timing, as always – Marja stops loving me. Just like that! Pass the salt, put up umbrella, stop loving Maciek. She has no reason. She is sad, of course; she does not like hurting me. This turns everything upside down, this business of her saying *pozegnalny* to me. I am not finished loving her yet! But I cannot be angry with her. I can't *not* love her. She is still beautiful to me.

Can there be love with no pain? I used to think yes; for me, love was easy. Now I think not. I was stupid! And now I don't like love. It is not a friend.

I hear, from my cousins, that Marja she lives with a man called Tomas, of Jablonowskich family. Marja loves this man, Tomas, and of course he must be loving her too. He must hear that terrible way she sings, and still want to kiss her. I don't know. Maybe he loves her because she makes him think of his mama.

I think love is like songs. Beginning, middle and end. Some love lives have long middles, with big crescendos and a final solo. A widower or widow, feeling restless, learning to sleep in middle of bed. Some songs just stop, for no reason. A three-minute pop song that at first you play, play, play. Then suddenly, one day you hear this song, lalala, while you are making cup of tea, or brushing teeth, and you want to vomit. For me, the song never got old. For Marja . . . vomit.

Some mornings when I wake, at first I cannot believe I am here, like this. Not in my old office at the college. Not with her. I never thought my life would be having this shape. Don't get me wrong. I am not bored with my jobs here. You think my work sounds menial? Below me? Well, I have to tell you a secret: I can hardly keep up with it. Everything in the world is so puzzling, *so miraculous*, every minute of every day. You think I am strange? I think everyone is strange. I think the world is strange. It's the strangest place in the world. Who cares? It is the world, no matter what I think. That being one of the things I love – that the world is itself. Not me.

Ciotka Agata says that I waste my life here, that I should use my education. But why does she think my life has this value? I am not special. And all jobs are equal, for a philosopher.

'Your pizza, it is ready now,' I tell the woman with four children.

I go around the counter and go outside because she can't hear my shout.

'It is ready now. Your pizza.'

'Oh! The pizza! Our lovely pizza!' and she laughs because she's forgotten the pizza. The children scream, they are so excited. They dance! Who would think that pizza cause such excitement?

I think at first, that I will keep going north until I come to a very small island. I want to be alone. But in the end, I am tired. I feel old. I stop when I come to this place. It is a good place. But for me, Ross-shire could be anywhere.

And there are thousands of Poles here, you must have noticed. It makes this place seem not so far from home. I have some friends now, men who also came from Krakow to work, and we always say hello and smile. They are much younger. One day I'll invite them to eat with me.

Some man, he wants fish and chips. I tell him to go to fish and chip shop next door. I only make pizza. A little girl and her little sister want a mini ham and pineapple. Their faces are sticky with sweets. The big sister, she cannot be six. A very old man, he wants a medium spicy. The girls stare at him. He has big bulgy things on his neck, and hairs that walk out of his nostrils.

It starts to rain, and he is here again.

'Hello,' I say and smile. 'It is you again, Sam.'

'Aye, it's me.' He smiles too, but just a little smile. He always has a little smile, never a big one. And his eyes, no smile at all.

I give the pizzas to the little girls and man, and they leave. I remember the first time Sam comes. A few weeks ago. School lunchtime, place busy. He doesn't stand in the queue, just stands by the window, and when the kids leave, he still stands and looks out window. A little guy. He doesn't look at me, and I ask if he is late for school.

'Nah,' he said, like he is way too old for school.

He says my name wrong for a long time. I understand. There is no place in your mouth for words you only hear one time.

'You want to work in here on Saturdays, Sam? Just a few hours. Maybe noon to three.'

And I get a big smile, first time. And then, it is like his smile pulls beauty into Pizza Palace, because here she is!

She's the woman I watch swim up and down every Tuesday, up and down for half an hour, and she doesn't splash or talk or smile to any of the other women. Just breaststrokes up and down, quietly, like a contemplating mermaid. It's my job to watch her; I'm the pool attendant Tuesdays and Thursdays. I watch all the swimmers, but she the most. Her perfect head never in the water, her eyes like she is very far away. I know she feels like nobody does see her, and she is thinking: I am alone. Look at her! She has nothing wrong with her. No thing. She is Snow White. Same white skin, same red lips, same blue eyes.

What is she doing here in my Pizza Palace?

'Hello, I can help you?' I know my face is not right because she gives me a look. Then she opens her mouth and says:

'Can I have a mushroom mini, please. Thank you very much.'

This is the first time I hear her voice. It is like her swim. It's like . . . she doesn't want to splash the air. She breaststrokes the air in my Pizza Palace, and this air, it moves over me like the calm waves from some place, some beach on the Baltic Sea. Whoosh! A door has just opened in my chest, and a sea gust blows in. No, this is not a nice feeling. It is very far from nice.

'Yes, that is good. Five minutes,' I say.

'Fine,' she says, and then no one knows what to do. I know I must begin to make the pizza, but she stands there and she looks at me. Maybe she recognises me? Sam makes a noise with the brush, but it is a far away noise. The shop window is huge, practically the whole wall, and looks onto the high street. The rain is suddenly hard against this window. Is it hail? I can hear thunder, and a carrier bag flies by the window with a woman chasing it. This is like something that happens in movies. It is very odd but true. In this tilting moment, I feel Marja fall away from me. There she goes! I can still see her, but now she is just a woman

I used to love in Krakow. As if my heart has a limited love capacity, room for one love only. Pulling swim woman in, it releases Marja.

Swim woman – *what is her name?* – finally turns to stare out the window at the storm, and I turn to make her pizza. The best pizza I can make.

Sam

I stare at Maciek; Maciek stares at Mrs MacLeod. Mrs MacLeod stares out the window.

After she leaves with her mushroom mini, I say:

'She's got a husband, you know. They live up Swordale Road.'

He looks at me stupid-like, but Maciek lives in Evanton too, so he knows fine where Swordale Road is. I've been to his caravan twice now. It's like two minutes from my house. Last time I went, he had my favourite biscuits – isn't that nice? My own parents never remember to get mint KitKats.

Not told them about Maciek. Totally know what they'd say. Think I'm daft? They'd say he was a perv, and I'd not to go there. A man. A foreigner. Must be up to no good, inviting schoolboys to his caravan.

Like the paranoid saddos they are.

It's totally obvious Maciek's into women, not schoolboys. Always checking the ladies out. You should see the way girls eyeball him in the shop. Nice ass, I heard one of them whisper to her pal. And he so flirts with them. He acts quiet, but he's a total slapper. In a good way.

I want to be a slapper too. Up for it.

Bit weird, him fancying Mrs MacLeod. She's a bit posh. And tidy, not in good way. Not to mention totally married. He's still looking like he's been hit on the head.

'She's married to my English teacher. Mr MacLeod.'

'What? What are you saying?' He squints, as if he's just waking.

'Mr MacLeod. Took my phone off me last week. Prick.'

'Who?'

'Ah, forget it. Never mind.' I put the brush away, and check my hair. Maciek has this little mirror at the back.

'Ok, I am never minding.'

'See you Saturday, ok Maciek?'

'Yes, that will be good Sam.'

I like Maciek, he is probably my best friend right now, and he seems pretty smart and all. But all the way home on the bus I keep thinking: Crap, why would Maciek want to shag Mr MacLeod's missus? She's not even got tits.

OCTOBER

Evanton

Just as every day is a whole life, with a birth, middle and death, every person in this town is the whole human race. And families that appear solid are sometimes not, and broken individuals are sometimes whole.

Sometimes, on a windless night, or very early still dawn, you can hear Evanton breathe. A little asthmatic in the winter maybe, a little irregular in the spring. But there is a heart to this place and the beat never stops.

When the new Millennium Bridge opened in London, they had to close it after a day because of dangerous swaying. What the fancy paid engineers had not taken into consideration, is that people in a group tend to move in tandem after about five seconds. When this causes a wobble, they all adjust their walking again to compensate, hence making the wobble wobblier. Evantonians do this too. New comers, locals, old and young. They all go off to school and their jobs every day, but when they come home, after three seconds, their hearts synchronise. It does not matter if they even know or notice each other. Listen. Ba boom! Ba boom! Ba boom! Ba boom!

When an Evantonian falls in love, like Maciek has and Ania will, the beat takes on a manic note for at least three weeks. Generally, it is good for the village when the heartbeat becomes audible, though it never lasts.

Ania

Pregnant women everywhere, suddenly. Five of them in the changing rooms, their bellies in various stages of being stretched. I am still singular, despite scheduled uses of fertile times. Very weird scanty period, but still a period. I've never had sex so often. I am not complaining. I am not a complainer by nature – I take responsibility for my life.

Baby-making sex is different. It appeals to my sense of utility. There is no waste in the act now. Today is the first day of my fertile cycle. I expect to conceive within the week.

I am swimming right now, trying to find the mindless hypnotic rhythm that always soothes me. I can't. The music doesn't help. I swim over to the lifeguard to tell him. Who is he? I've seen him somewhere else before. Aside from his lifeguard seat. He doesn't stare directly at my breasts, but he wants to. Something in his unfocused glance at my approaching shoulders and neck. I can feel his would-be stare. My swimming costume is as modest as it can be – one piece, black – but still my breasts feel his stare that is not a stare, as if the swimming costume is not there.

'Do you think we could have classical music sometimes? Or . . . opera?' I ask him. 'Just now and then. Instead of Radio One.'

'Yes!' he says. 'I understand this perfectly,' he says, and I can tell he doesn't. Perhaps not used to speaking English. 'You like music?'

His teeth are extraordinarily white and straight, and his black eyes have as much of a lower lid as an upper lid. His eyebrows are heavy, and march across his brow. A raven in flight, above his eyes.

Latvian perhaps, or Lithuanian or Polish. There are suddenly so many of them around. I find them exotic, though they look like us. And even though I shouldn't. I've been surrounded by Poles all my life. Dad's been here since 1944, far longer than he was ever in Poland. He seems so old these days – well, I suppose he is old. He could be my grandfather. Ian thinks that having such old parents and being an only child has made me old for my age. Old fashioned. Perhaps. I hate rock music, don't like it when people swear or smoke or get drunk. I remember feeling impatient, often, and irritated with my classmates; happier when my peers reached adulthood. I probably know most of the people in Evanton, but I haven't been inside many houses. Not sat around many kitchen tables, and that's how I like it. I've heard of how village life can be, with cruel gossip and cliques, but I live in a village and never notice these things. I choose not to.

I raise my voice to this lifeguard who may be Polish or Lithuanian or Ukrainian. I push him some distance away from my breasts, with my clear voice and direct look.

'Yes, I like music. Not so much Radio One music. If I bring some CDs from home next Tuesday, can you play them here?'

'Ah! Yes, please bring these things.'

He is the man from Pizza Palace. I remember. An odd frozen moment, after I told him which pizza I wanted. I stare at the nametag on his shirt. Maciek. Maciek.

'You can say it like it is magic you are saying. *Magic*,' he says.

I blush.

'Magic?'

'Yes, this is right. Magic is my name.'

If this man who is not Scottish wants to not look at my breasts, well, maybe my breasts will not look right back. Un-looked at, my breasts tingle as I re-enter the pool. Another ten laps, then home to Ian, and baby-making. I have a plan, and it involves a late summer birth, and six months leave of absence from work. Then weaning and childminder finding and weekends spent cooking and freezing lots of healthy baby food. I've already bought the miniature plastic containers. I have a list, with things like investigate savings accounts for children, contact childminder association, Montessori schools, buy early learning tapes for French, vitamins for myself, oils for my skin, baby carriers on Ebay.

The next night, I am back in my tiny office, my marriage mending room. I'm twenty minutes early. I open my notebook and glance at my old list to see if there is anything I can add. Marriage is a subject like any other, like geography or history, and I read the existing research and take my own notes.

About two dozen pages are excerpts from studies on marriage rituals, statistics on divorce, fidelity, comparative cultural differences, i.e. Chinese domestic violence versus domestic violence in Italy. And information on the vaginal orgasm as opposed to clitoral orgasms, and their connection to rates of stress-related conditions. Statistics, of course, can be gathered and interpreted any way you need, in order to support whatever conviction you have. That's the beauty of them – whatever you suspect is true, there'll be some statistic to pat you on the shoulder and say: Yup! Right again!

Personally, I favour the Relate study that says 58% of clients report improvements after counselling.

And then the lists, which are spread over eight pages to make room for deletions and additions, of which there are a lot. In fact, I will need to buy a new notebook soon, and transcribe these.

Reasons Why People Fall in Love

1. Sex. To keep human race going. Eggs shouting to be fertilised. Pheromones screaming.

2. Shared interests. Bird watching. Black and white films. Feeling understood.
3. Timing. Desert island theory. If there are just three people, you will fall in love with one of them.
4. Loneliness. Nature hates a vacuum, sucks people into voids.
5. Genetic predilection. Like hayfever. Tendency to infatuate.
6. Near death experiences. Feeling mortal. Wartime mentality.
7. The right person theory. Accidental. Meet that right person, and bam!

Reasons Why People Marry

1. Desire to have legitimate babies. Start an empire.
2. Safety.
3. Socially respectable. Good for careers and dinner parties.
4. Financially sound.
5. In order to release themselves from the time-consuming process of courting.
6. Simply in order to be a husband or wife. Belong to someone.
7. Because a baby is already on the way.
8. To please their families.

Reasons Why People Divorce

1. Boredom. A need for intensity.
2. Infidelity. Symptom of misery, or cause of misery.
3. Mid-life crisis. Mortality looming, etc.
4. Loss of desire. Can lead to number 2.
5. Incompatibility. Grown apart.
6. Curiosity. To see what divorce is like. Related to number 1.
7. Self-esteem. Not liking the self they are in the marriage.
8. Because they can imagine a better relationship.

Reasons Why People Stay Married

1. Children.
2. Laziness.
3. Cowardice.

4. Stubbornness.
5. Shared history.
6. Financial ease.
7. To please their families.
8. Shared friends & routines.
9. To sleep next to someone.
10. To have a witness to their lives.
11. Fear of loneliness.
12. Fear of the unknown.
13. Habit.
14. Because they simply like marriage. It suits them. Happiness is irrelevant.

The list of reasons to stay married remains the longest. And yet, I believe there is as much benefit to parting as remaining together. Despite appearances, I am not a marriage evangelist. Some lives are ruined by remaining together. Some people act as if they had a dozen other lives to live and don't mind wasting one or two. Some couples are good for fifty years, while others stubbornly refuse to part, decades after their sell-by date. As if there will be some kind of reward, like Tesco vouchers, for loyalty.

Oh! I've just noticed I've omitted the word love from all these lists. How could that be? Theoretically, loving someone could even be a reason for leaving them. Liberating someone from hell because you care about them. I can't believe that never occurred to me. I scribble love, love, love, love on the lists – even the list of reasons to fall in love. People fall in love because they are in love with love!

Is love ever the same for people? Would they even recognise it, if they could for a second feel what was inside another heart? What that person calls love, they may think is . . . indigestion. Or a burst of crazy joy. Or just a frightened feeling, a not-wanting-to-be-alone feeling. Romantic love is not much to do with marriage, and so officially not my concern really. The nature of, the cause of, the purpose of romantic love – no idea. Lust is all that's needed to propagate the race, so why all the poetry?

I do have, however, a page titled:

Ways to Ensure the Longevity of Romantic Love

1. Die young.
2. Live apart.
3. Live during a major war or natural catastrophe.
4. One or both of you be unavailable.
5. Love someone who does not know you exist.
6. Do not consummate it, but have at least one amazing kiss.
7. Do not speak the same language.
8. Conduct the romance in a foreign country, where you cannot stay long.

My list of *Rules for Successful Marriage* is the shortest of all. It used to be the longest, but it has been whittled down to:

1. Be polite.
2. Have regular sex.

There is also a page with a list of quotes:

Love is the delightful interval between meeting a beautiful girl, and discovering she looks like a haddock.

- *John Barrymore*

Love: a temporary insanity cured by marriage.

- *Hemingway*

It's possible to love a human being if you don't know them too well.

- *Charles Bukowski*

Love is the triumph of imagination over intelligence.

- *H.L. Mencken*

Marriage is the triumph of habit over hate.

- *Charles Schultz*

Marriage is like paying an endless visit in your worst clothes.

- J.B. Priestely

Marriage is the only adventure open to the cowardly.

- Voltaire

Marriage: a souvenir of love.

- Helen Rowland

Pretty cynical, most of them – but then, they are all writers. Writers are melodramatic, notoriously promiscuous and melancholic. Everyone knows this.

Not everyone falls in love; some people fall in love just once, and some people fall in love continuously. People in love often think of themselves as innocent, helpless. They tend to do what they like without apology or rational explanation, as if love is a virus. And getting over break-ups – it really is like getting over the flu. You think you are all better, then one morning you wake up coughing. People tell me everything, so I know these things are true. One week they are hunky dory, the next there's tears again.

7:56.

I put the book away, and shut my eyes for a minute.

Please, I whisper as usual into this empty room.

Please help me keep my heart open and show them the way to keep their hearts open. Let love re-enter their lives, whether they remain together or part. Let anger and pettiness fall away, and dignity and generosity enter.

Thank you.

Amen.

And right on time, there's the bell, and Rose and Harry. Interesting how people who have not had time for each other in years become prompt suddenly. Fear slows down time, and panic nearly stops it. Most of all, fear wakes us up to the passing of time. All the couples I see are so awake, they're exhausted.

Rose

God, I'm so fucking shattered. I've lost the hang of sleeping altogether.

Listen to me, like an idiot:

'Hello Ania! How are you? You look great, I love that sweater. Monsoon? Almost bought it myself. Perfect colour.' Followed by me giggling, in a stupid fake way. As if I'm here for an intimate dinner party, but am not too sure if the hostess likes me enough. Fuck, I hate myself.

'Evening,' says Harry, more sombrely. 'How are you? Good, good.'

Once upstairs, and seated, Ania puts her hands together like she's about to pray, and asks:

'So, how has it been? How did it go?'

'The sex?' blurts Harry.

'Well, if you like. How did the love-making go?' she says, in her practical way. As if she is asking about the outcome of a difficult recipe.

'Didn't happen,' grunts Harry like a sulky adolescent. 'Knew it wouldn't. Not surprised, really.'

'Oh? Rose?'

'Oh, she hates sex. With me, anyway.'

'Harry, let Rose answer, please. You will have your chance to contribute soon.'

'Sorry, go ahead. Tell her, Rose.'

'Rose?'

Ania is like our head teacher, I suddenly realise. The same superiority, the same lack of humour. And this is definitely a lasagne day. I feel like saying to her: So, you've got a good job, a good man, a nice house? It can still all go tits up, lady.

'Ok, I'm sorry,' I say, as if I'm anything but sorry. 'Sorry, if I don't think sex is the answer to everything. Sex is only one part of marriage, anyway. It's like a really very small part, after twenty-two years. All my married friends say the same thing.'

'You're right, Rose. Sex is important, but it is just one part. What are the other parts of your marriage?'

God she is so fucking even-toned and conciliatory! But I give it a try:

'Marriage is, well, it's hard to separate it all out, after two decades. There's Sam, of course. We were married almost eight years before he was born, he was a well wanted baby. But there's also the photo albums, our group of friends.'

'Who all live in Leith,' interrupts Harry.

'Yes, well, but they're still our friends.'

'Are they?'

Hmmm . . . it's true, our marital crisis had an odd effect on our circle. We never said much to anyone, but people knew. You know what people are like. Everything started to change. That's one of the reasons it was easy to move. Our old life was gone forever anyway. Certainly our friendship with Alpin and his fucking lovely wife Sarah was fucked. I've got one new friend here, Lily – thank fuck – from the canteen, and she's a bit boring to tell the truth, but beggars can't be choosers. I'm useless without pals.

I'm going to email Alpin when I get home. To hell with this. What have I got to lose?

My heart is doing that thing again, all excited, just imagining re-connecting with him. It's like injecting adrenaline.

I clear my throat, focus on perfect-as-a-china-doll Ania. Jesus, whose stupid idea was it to try wanky Relate stuff? Oh yeah.

Mine. I am the boss of this marriage, and it's not over till I fucking say it is.

Get through the hour, I tell myself. Get through it. Think later. Email later. No! Yes! No!

'Well, it's true, people change,' I concede. 'But this time of trying to make new friends and a new life is a part of our marriage too. We're finding new rituals. Sunday walks on Kiltearn Beach, and the Wednesday night curry in Dingwall. It's all the knick knacks, all the furniture we've chosen together. It's the colour of the bathroom wall, the curtains in the sitting room.'

'That was your victory, Rose.'

For fuck's sake, I think.

'Harry!' warns Ania.

'You're right Harry, I won that battle and we have colour instead of glaring white, but my point is, the bathroom walls are now a marital anecdote.'

'And the curtains. Who chose them?'

'Oh Harry, you're missing the point.'

'Oh yeah, the point being that you get your way every time or you go into deep depression, a sulk, and it's hell being anywhere near you.'

By god, he's right. I'm a spoiled bitch. But what about the fact he is so boring and oblivious to me, I could die and he'd not notice till his tea didn't appear on the table? Is that not a crime? I'm about to mention this, when Ania says:

'Harry,' in her irritating soothing tone. 'Your resentment is very natural. Marriage is always a series of compromises. Always, and it may seem sometimes that you are making all the compromises. Let's finish listening to what Rose has to say about marriage.'

A pause, while Harry sighs. Ania sighs too. I take a breath and carry on.

'Anyway. It isn't just the stuff, the household stuff. There's all the memories too – all the memories of the fights as well as the good times. And the frightening times, and sad times, like your sister dying, my breast cancer scare. All the times we've lived through together. Marriage is all our stuff mixed up together; our messy car, our shared sock drawer. True, I think sex is overrated and you'd like a lot more, but maybe you don't get everything you want. Maybe no one gets both a nice stable married life and great sex.'

Harry looks unimpressed, out the dark window.

'Rose, I think you are perhaps settling for too little,' Ania says very gently. 'Good sex is possible even in forty-year-old marriages. It sounds like your marriage is a solid one, and there is only the problem with sex, yes? Would you consider sex therapy?'

Sex therapy? Is she insane?

'She's right!' rejoices Harry. 'Good sex can exist even in really old marriages!'

'What do you think, Rose?' asks the sadistic cow.

'No! Jesus! I am so tired of this attitude. Why *must* I enjoy sex with my husband? Why is it my fault if I don't? If Harry didn't fancy me enough to perform, if he was impotent, we'd all be whispering: It's ok Harry, don't worry, it doesn't really matter, Rose loves you anyway. Rose should lose weight, put on make up, try to seduce you. But if I'm not into it, I'm supposed to go to a therapist to get fixed, so Harry can get his nooky every night, and stop accusing me of being frigid.'

'Do you think you are frigid?' asks Ania.

'Frigid!' snorts Harry. 'Apparently not! Tell her Rose.'

'Harry, this has nothing to do with . . .'

'Tell her. It's why we moved from Leith. It's why we're here talking to Ania.'

'You don't need to say anything you are uncomfortable about saying, Rose.'

I give Harry my look. My *whatever* look. Under a smile, he shoots me back a look of utter contempt. It is all so quick, so natural, I almost smile. Our secret mutual hatred.

'Fine. About a year ago, a man kissed me. Harry'd been pissing me off, and I was a bit drunk. I was pretty up for it, I guess. So there was this kiss. An old friend. It was a short kiss, but proper

– an on the lips job – and no one but Harry had kissed me in so long I was kind of caught unawares, and it . . . well, it went right through me.'

'The kiss?'

'Great,' says Harry. 'I love this bit.'

'Harry,' warns Ania.

'You asked. That kiss undid me. It reminded me what kissing could be like. Used to be like.'

'Quite understandable. And quite common. Very few long-term marriages manage to avoid temptation. And did the kiss go any further?'

'Only in my fantasies.'

'Liar,' mumbles Harry.

'Alright. We met once, in the afternoon at his place, had a bottle of wine and bonked. And that was it. No big deal.'

Harry looks pleased to hear my crime again, out loud. Perv. And he still doesn't have a clue. The other times. Me falling in love. Wonder if I still have his email address? Didn't I delete it? Fuck.

'Anyway, he's not important. Kiss man.'

'Alpin,' says Harry, smugly.

'Yes, alright. Alpin. Alpin is not important.'

'You weren't in love with him?' asks Ania.

'No. Just a stupid crush.'

'Have you had crushes before?'

'Of course! Doesn't everyone? From age five.'

'But you understand the difference between that kind of untested infatuation, and a real relationship? The kind of love you feel for Harry. You do love Harry, don't you?' Ania asks this in a tone which says she is certain the answer is yes. Cow, cow, cow.

'Aye, of course I do,' I answer obediently.

'No, you don't,' whines Harry. 'You so don't love me!'

The famous pause you see in movies. The blush, the averted eyes that tell it all. We are way too good at this. Like we're reading a script.

'You're right. I don't love you, Harry.' Right then, seeing his face, I suddenly *do* love him. I must be insane. 'Sorry, I just don't.' I say, and I love him even more! My heart is expanding right into this room. What is wrong with me? I kind of giggle through my nose, a snort, and so does Harry after a second.

'Duh, you don't love me. Knew it,' he says, with a smirk.

We stop smirking and snorting, and a full minute passes. More staring at the floor and the wall. Someone should be videoing us. Reality television should use Relate. Big Broken-Hearted Brother. Or Harry could star in one of those shows like Jeremy Kyle, and the title would be: My Wife Only Wears Thongs For Other Men.

'Have you ever loved me?' whispers Harry, melodramatically.

I fight another urge to giggle, then shrug apologetically. Giggling time is over.

'Nah. Not really, I guess. Not properly, like a wife should.'

Harry makes a sound like I've punched him in the stomach, hard. A winded sound.

Shit. He didn't know that?

'In the beginning, I thought it would come later, and I really did try. I waited and waited for my heart to lift when you entered a room.'

'But it never did?'

'Nope. It never did. I gained weight, remember? If I'd been in love, I would've lost weight. Everyone knows that.'

'Jesus.'

'Ah Harry, we're friends right? We're married.'

'But *I* love *you*.'

Fuck off!

'Well la de da! You're functional and I'm not!' I am definitely going to find that email address and write Alpin tonight.

The air in the room is thick. Ania stands up and opens the window a crack.

'We seem to have reached a plateau not normally reached till at least the fifth session,' informs Ania in a level, slightly reproachful, voice. 'Why are you in a hurry to do this?'

Why indeed, are we even here? I almost say. And why haven't I slapped you yet?

When Ania sits down again, she commands both of our faces, holds our attention for a moment, and smiles her concluding smile. We sit like guilty children.

'The hour, I am afraid, is up,' she says.

As an afterthought, she adds:

'Please don't worry. The temporary absence of, or imbalance of love does not mean a marriage is dead.'

Die, bitch, die.

Maciek

Dead! A Polish girl. Listen to this: Some man, he kills her. They find her body in a park in Glasgow. She's on the front page of *The Press and Journal*, and though I only pick up this paper to practise reading English, I can't read now. Her face, it is smiling and she is very pretty and very young and she looks excited in this picture. Like it's Christmas tomorrow. Some man, he kills her and the police, they don't know who. Maybe it's someone she trusts. I can almost see how it will be with her parents. They say goodbye to her just two, three weeks ago. Hugs and tears and they joke with her about finding a rich Scottish husband, and she waves goodbye at the airport. And now they cannot believe this terrible thing. They trust Scotland to be a safe place.

And last week, there is another death, a Polish boy. Found dead on the A9. No one knows how. Police, they again ask for witnesses. Maybe he is drunk, walking home, falling into the road and a car hits him. Maybe he is dead already, and someone, they toss his body out of their car like a piece of rubbish. It is just a small story in the paper, not like this pretty girl who is dead. No front-page photograph of this boy. But this boy – he has a family too.

These Polish families, if they come here for the funeral, they will not know it's different here. In Poland, there are not so many flowers at funerals, but there are lots and lots of candles. And after the tears, there must be smiles and talk of good times. We know that to be sad is to hold back the soul. Too much crying, it's not what you do when you love somebody. Sadness weighs them down. Here, it is so different. They should take their children home.

I'm sitting in the Tesco café, trying to read *The Press and Journal*, trying not to worry about grieving Polish families, and I'm drinking very bad coffee. I tried the tea, but it also tastes bad. Home, it is never tea bags, always loose black tea with raspberry juice, and sometimes a small pour of vodka in this sweet tea. It is possible I may work here in Tesco one day. There are shelves devoted to Polish food, and I noticed some Poles working here already. One very pretty girl at the tills, I think her name is Brinski. I hope she doesn't have bad luck like this girl in Glasgow. I hope she is careful, and doesn't trust every man she meets.

Ratunku! There is my contemplating mermaid! Mini mushroom pizza woman with whitest skin and bluest eyes!!! She's sitting a beret's throw away, on her perfect bottom. I notice when I walk over to get more sugar for my terrible coffee.

'Please! Hello, how are you?'

She smiles and says: 'I'm fine, how are you?' Her smile is small and cold, yes, but it is still a smile. I think she does not remember me.

'I make you pizza sometimes, and I play your CD, your opera, at the swimming pool. Where you swim. All Tuesdays.'

'So you are! Maciek, is it not?'

'Yes. You're saying my name the right way. Thank you.' I make a small bow, take off my hat.

'It's an unusual name. I like your hat.'

'Ah! Thank you.' I look at my very old hat. 'It is very old. It was my uncle's. When he wasn't dead. He let me play with it when I was a boy. Now, if it's not on my head, I miss it.'

'What's it called? A trilby?'

'Yes, I think that is the word in English.'

She tilts her head, and looks at me. 'Hats do make one feel different,' says this angel with angel's red lips. It is easy to love her and I do this thing. Love her. But I move the talk on.

'I think, I think it depends on my mood,' I tell her. 'Some days, my hat holds my thoughts in, or they fly away.' I do something with my fingers, like they are foofing my thoughts into the Tesco café air.

She smiles and looks back to her book, but I can tell. I know she wants to know more. She wants to know where I am from.

'I am from Poland. You know Poland? From Krakow.'

'Ah! Well, I've heard that's a lovely city.'

'It is a very nice place, yes. You like this coffee? It is terrible coffee, no? I have to drink many cups. Many,' I tell her with a very sad face.

She laughs, even though I do not make a joke. Oh! What a laugh. I can tell she doesn't do this laugh often. It is an amateur laugh. Her mouth is so pink, and her laugh it is very pink too. Her laugh makes me hard. Then she says:

'I'm drinking tea. Is the coffee so terrible?'

'Yes,' I say, with the very serious face still so she will laugh again. 'Terrible, but not as terrible as the tea. How can you drink it? At home I drink no thing but tea, but here . . .' Then because I cannot stop looking at her, and she is looking right at my eyes, I say:

'I will buy you a coffee right now. So you'll know how very terrible it is.'

'Oh! Oh!' Her face is now pink. So many pinks! It is good to watch. Like sunrise. Like porn.

'You wait, I get. One minute only.' I rip my eyes from her face. Ouch!

When I bring back the coffee, she's still pink and I don't sit next to her. I know when to not be close.

'Here,' I say. 'Try this. You see for yourself.' Then I go back to my own seat and pick up the newspaper again. Pretend I am this busy man.

I can feel her behind me, drinking the coffee I buy for her.

Already I feel ridiculous. I can feel her, and the words on the page are just black marks, not words with meaning at all. Why did I buy her a coffee, when she is drinking tea?

'Thank you,' she says to my back.

I turn only a little. I do not want to frighten this woman. She will think I am stupid. How can she know who I am, when I cannot speak to her in Polish? But I have the manners:

'You are welcome. Of course.' I nod, and tip my hat again. She might think I'm stupid, but polite. A gentleman!

I read and she sips. I know she looks at me. She likes my shoulders, I think. My neck. I think of something she'd like to know. I turn and smile. And then I say to her:

'You must know that today, it is All Souls Day.'

'Halloween? That was yesterday.'

'Maybe yes, but today is All Souls Day, and at my home the cemeteries will be full of candles in candle jars. *Znicze*. Not flowers, but many little lights.'

'Oh!' She says oh! a lot. She looks at me carefully. Actually, she is careful all the time, about everything. I can't imagine her drunk, or falling, or spilling. I love her, so I love this too. Or maybe I love this caution, and so I love her? Who cares! My heart fills like a huge pink balloon.

'Please. You think I am just telling you a story, but it is true. And I think, well I think it is very beautiful. I wish I could be there tonight. And I wish you could see, too. You would not believe it.'

I try with words and my hands and my eyes, to make this beautiful picture go into her head.

'The whole place, candles on graves. There is a sweet smell, from bees wax. And sometimes there are flame fleas.'

'It sounds magical,' she says politely. Then her face, it changes. As if a candle suddenly lights up inside her.

'Fireflies!' she says. 'You mean fireflies!' And though there are no fireflies in this country, I know that now she sees the candles in *znicze*.

'When the Pope dies, the Polish Pope, some streets inside Warsaw have candles on the ground that spell out *Totus Tuus*, which means All Yours.'

She doesn't say anything, just looks at me. Sweet, sweet woman! Then she smiles and says:

'I love candles.'

'*Ja tez*,' I say. 'I think candles, they make everything a mystery.'

Then because we do not know each other well yet, I feel this is enough, and I do a small nod and turn around again. After a short time, maybe two minutes, I hear her chair and she is standing up and putting on her coat. I do not turn. I turn a page of newspaper. I am mister refrigerator.

'I don't know,' she says as she passes me. 'I didn't think the coffee was that bad.'

I cannot answer; all the words I know in English are gone. I can see she is trying very hard not to smile. That smile she hides – it is big, and I, Maciek, give her that smile. She wants me to shake her boodles, of course.

'And what is your name?' I say to the back of her head, which is hiding the smile.

She turns around fast, not smiling, looks right at me and says:

'Ania. My name is Ania.'

And then there's her smile, out again like a sudden rainbow. Like she has pulled her jumper off and her bra, it is sexy black lace.

I am shocked. Ania is not a name I expect to hear. What is it doing in her mouth?

And I slip into a hole. You think you are walking along a flat road, you think about what to cook for dinner, if you need to buy milk, if you will ever fuck a woman again, if the coffee can get worse. And you think you know how the whole day will be, because you walk this road many times. Every day. Then suddenly whoomph! Into a deep hole you fall. Down, down, down.

Tonight I light a candle to protect me from falling. I set this candle by the photograph of Mamusia, who is in the middle of a conversation with someone. Listen. There is a thing they do at home, not so much anymore, but in some places a baby is still given a candle at baptism. It is lit and the priest blesses it with holy water. And this same candle is lit again on the first communion and the confirmation. And when this person dies, this same candle, their own candle, is lit one last time and put in their folded hands. Like this.

I wish I had a candle like this. My own candle, to be lit on all the important days, and on any day I need it. I think a candle can keep loneliness away. Of course I am afraid of being alone in the dark. Aren't you?

NOVEMBER

Evanton

The year has closed down. The commuters drive home in the dark, some to rooms well lit and warm and peopled, some to dark cold rooms waiting for their flick of the switch. And the women in the shop comment on how Guy Fawkes has fallen on a Sunday this year, and they tisk, as if it has been careless to stray so far from a convenient day. A school night! A Sunday! The towns and cities have held the fireworks on Saturday night, but there is no forgetting the actual night, and teenagers are already making their way down to the beach in the drizzle, lugging carrier bags of bottles and firewood. Some of the more sensible have tents and sleeping bags, knowing that half their friends will be piling into their tents later. Adults of all ages drift down too, some with small children on their shoulders. Maciek is there, with Sam. Ian and Ania walk down, and later Rose and Harry. Three bonfires, close together, are lit; no reason, an accident. People piling up wood in different places. The wind is fickle and blows sparks and smoke in shifting directions, so everyone except the very drunk keeps on the move. From the old bridge, by the derelict church and churchyard, the dark shapes around the fires look mysterious, ancient. They look all of a piece. No one can look at them without wishing they were part of the group; no one can even think of them without yearning for something nameless. So even the shop women, separately, in their own houses, get out their anoraks and umbrellas and head down to the beach.

Everyone on the beach is connected, in ways that would seem ridiculous in fiction. Nicole in the shop's father really is having an affair with her worst enemy's auntie, whose house is cleaned by Nicole's little cousin Amy, and Nicole's mother's best friend is the mother of Tommy, who gave Nicole her first proper kiss, but then he shagged one of her pals, who is now at the bonfire, within inches of all these people. And everything that ever happened in Evanton is still echoing, like skeletons preserved in peat bogs, only not powerless.

The weather is vile.

And the next day, also vile.

Sam

There's this new girl, and she's quite fit. Polish. Her dad drops her off by the lights, he's got this major tinky van, but she always looks good. Roksana. *Roksana.* Cool name.

First off, I totally understand how she feels, because three months ago I was the new kid. As if going from primary to secondary wasn't shite anyway, like sending babies out to play on the A9, being a new kid is fucking shite.

But she's cool. She knows how you got to act, to not get killed. I can tell she knows you need to find the line. Stay out of people's way. Not upset anyone. Figure out the cliques. Only be noticed for cool stuff, like being funny, or good at something not geeky. Be fun to be around. You got to give people a reason to like you. And no matter what anyone tells you, people like it when you look good. No one is so not shallow that they don't think that, even if they tell themselves looks don't matter. You got to work at it, and hide the fact you're working on it. And Roksana does. She's sound.

She's hanging with my group, the good-looking crowd. We're a big group, so it's more open. She's smart at maths, so she's in my class with Miss Reid, who's a skive. She likes Roksana cause her homework is always done on time, and she gets high marks on her tests. But then at least once a week, Roksana chats too much to the girl next to her and gets told off, and when she does it twice during the class, she gets a letter to her parents. That is how she is so cool. She understands you got to be good and bad at the right times. Invisible and noticed. Walk the line. I'm well impressed.

She's hot also, which helps. She has these eyes, like they are sleepy all the time. Very blonde hair, almost white. And her skin is very white too, zero spots. Her lips are a bit like Megan Fox's. Fat and red and sexy. She is almost two years older than me because they start school later in Poland, but she's wee. Way shorter than me. Everyone can see she's fit. Look at her! Not that I think about her all the time. I have a life. Just getting through my days, avoiding freaks and pervs and pricks, takes all my energy. And then I go home to my tight-ass gay parents.

But here's the thing: If Roksana's late, I find myself watching the door for her. And once, when she didn't come at all, I spent the whole class with this feeling, like where is she? And later that night, I was watching *Top Gear*, but really I was wondering if she was sick, and if she was sick, was she in bed, and if she was in bed, was she reading or napping or watching a film? And was she wearing a sexy see-through nightie or some stupid kiddie jammies?

So I get this plan.

'Maciek, would you teach me some Polish?'

We're eating some cake that Maciek calls sandy cake, and I call marble cake. We're in his caravan, which pongs.

Maciek laughs. 'Of course I teach you. We can start now if you want. If you meet someone, you might say: *Czesc, jak leci*? It means: Hi, how are you?'

'Chejyuk, geelegge?'

'Almost,' he says kindly. He's cool. Maciek's a bit old, but he *is* cool. 'We will try again.'

Polish sounds a bit like English, only played backwards, faster. It does! Listen next time you're near people speaking Polish. It's so hard to speak. We practise and practise, till I figure a way to remember words for things like tea and apple and how are you.

It reminds me of the time I took piano lessons, and was boab till the day my fingers seemed to suddenly understand what to do. Learning Polish feels physical, and makes me sleepy.

'Remember you tell me about a teacher at your school, and his wife is buying a pizza from me?'

'The one who took my phone off me? Mr MacLeod. Cunt.'

'Ah, so that is the name. I am very bad with Scottish names still. MacLeodcunt.'

'MacLeod. Not the cunt bit.'

'Ok! MacLeod only. Ok.'

'Why?' I ask. 'Why are you wondering about him?'

'Just I am wondering. No real reason.'

Maciek is so lying. He is a crap liar. Then he teaches me some Polish swears. You can never know enough insults, so I write them down. But I'm never going to use them with Roksana. She's not like that. I bet her family even go to church.

Ania

From my counselling room, I can see the top of St Mary's. I'm early, and noticing my view. My father used to take me there, to Mass. Some Sundays there would only be a dozen of us, and we'd spread out in the pews, to make us seem more. It was lonely and embarrassing, being Catholic here. Like going to parties that no one else wants to go to, and you feel sorry for the host.

I wonder if all these new Poles are going to St Mary's now. Maybe it is not so lonely when there are a lot of them. But they will think our church is so dull. So lacking in gilt and drama. Highlanders make shy Catholics. We don't have the weather for Catholicism.

Do you want to hear a secret? I miss being a Catholic.

But I have kept the praying habit, and I light candles too. I find it calming to silently consider the mystery of life. I light candles to invite a baby to join us. Then I pretend I am pregnant right now. An embryo is a promise of a human being. A minuscule collection of cells, rapidly and robustly and blindly spinning inside me. Like geese flying south, following memory imbedded in their DNA, but this scrap of humanity is a million times more miraculous. How does it know what complex processes to follow? How does each cell know whether to aim for becoming an ear lobe or a piece of lung? There is a soul already, of course. What is a soul, when you are not really Catholic anymore, just a former

Catholic who still lights candles? It is a pulse of electricity to jump-start a personality. It is a throb, a spark, a light for an eye not yet formed. It is love with nothing else attached to it.

Listen to me! Perhaps I should be a priest. Not a Relate counsellor, but a spiritual healer for the love forsaken. Yes. When I imagine standing in the pulpit, I fill with a confidence and warmth. My congregation would be all my clients. All the couples, like Rose and Harry, and the individuals whose partners have given up and will not come. Perhaps there is no difference between sad couples and sad individuals. Loneliness is in everyone, and no amount of marriage can alter the fact that we are all alone when we die.

I would write weekly sermons on love and dignity, and deliver them with a gentle urgency. I would wear soft, flowing dresses from that posh shop in Beauly. A wave of emotion would sometimes overcome my flock, and at some point there would be the spontaneous reaction. A loud burst of relieving tears. An involuntary shout of: Yes! Thank you! I feel the love!

The church would become humid with desire, and people would begin kissing each other, and hugging, and more. Like that poem by Roger McGough, all the white mothball bodies doing naughty things on the bus when the world was going to end at lunchtime. A few couples would no doubt drop to the floor between the pews, and tear at each other's clothing till flesh met flesh.

The whole place would thrum with the noise of bodies meeting bodies and the sound of loneliness fleeing out the door.

What is romantic love? Despite centuries of literature and essays claiming otherwise, it is something there are no words to describe. Language turns love into something that can only be anticipated or observed in the past tense. In my church, my sermon will aim for mindless thrumming, quiet embraces and heated silence. No thinking. No words.

Of course it is possible I am wrong about love. Where is my notebook?

Certainties about Love

1. Everyone wants to love (whether they know it or not).
2. Everyone wants to be loved (whether they know it or not).
3. Love can't be forced or faked.

Maciek played a new CD last night at the pool. Not one of my CDs. I didn't recognize it, but there was a violin in it that seemed to weep, and under that, a flute that kept rising. When it finished, I wanted to hear it again. But he did not put it on. He did not look at me, or even not-look at me. It made me feel strange. Since the Tesco meeting, I was starting to feel like we are kind of friends. Then he put on a Beatles CD, an old one. She loves you, yeah, yeah, yeah. My parent's music, really, but I like it. Makes me happy.

I had another period; a very light one again. I'm still not pregnant and sex with Ian is starting to resemble a chore, of the list variety. As in clean the toilet, pay gas bill, go to dentist. And I experienced a strange, very unpleasant sensation, when I saw Maciek last night. Nauseous. And dizzy. Wonder if I am becoming allergic to the chlorine? And his indifference was weirdly maddening. And my breasts. Even though my period has just past, they are pre-period swollen.

Oh! There is the doorbell already. I am so tired. I breathe in deeply, breathe out. Rose and Harry are in dire need of help. *Please help me.*

Rose

Help! Ania's apricot bloody room again. It's been an insane month, lasting several months, and yet here we are again already. We sit in the chairs we chose on the first night. We're creatures of habit, trying to break the habit of marriage. Life is change, and it hurts to change. Maybe that's all it boils down to.

All of life is like school, when you think about it. You might think you've got a spouse, or a parent, or a bossy friend or a Relate counsellor – but really they're just your teacher, and you're sitting in a puddle of pee, too scared to tell her. And you come back the next day, because that's the rule.

So here we are again, even though I would rather be cleaning up puke. Ania doesn't look quite as perfect as always, which cheers me slightly. Her face is flushed in an unattractive way, and there's something nervous in the way she's sitting. Perched forward, hands kind of clenched against each other. I wonder if there'll be an email from Alpin when I get home. I wonder if he's read mine yet. I wonder what he's doing right now. I think about the way it began again. With me emailing: *Are you there?* And him emailing back a minute later: *Yes! God, yes!*

'So tell me,' Ania says. 'How are things? Harry?'

She always asks him first.

'Fine, fine. You know. Work that's soul-destroying. Son who only mumbles. Badly cooked dinners, followed by cheap alcohol, telly, bed with frigid wife. Brilliant month.' His voice is deadpan, suicidal. I have to hand it to Harry. I am pretty good, but he is the pro of sarkiness.

'Oh dear,' says Ania, looking confused.

I start laughing and then Harry laughs too. In a high-pitched hysterical way, but still, it feels good to laugh. Finally Ania laughs and we stop laughing. Once she gets the joke, it's no longer funny.

'How have you been, Rose?'

I sigh dramatically – my speciality.

'You really want to know?'

'Yes, of course. You can be perfectly honest, please.'

I say: Well, a bit better, now I'm back in touch with my squeeze. *Not.*

'Not great. I miss Leith. Bit homesick. I don't really have any friends here yet, or . . .'

'What about Lily? You're always out with her these days,' whines Harry. Like he cares that I have a drink with Lily a few nights a week. She's not single, but her man works offshore, so she's basically on her own.

'True, I have a laugh with Lily some days, so what? I'm allowed to have one friend, and still feel low, aren't I? Anyway, times with her are pretty dire. She smokes like a chimney, and goes on and on about her grandchildren. Makes me mental sometimes.' Saying this I know I should feel disloyal. But nope. I am too depressed for guilt. The only times I am not depressed are the minutes spent emailing him.

I start telling her about how frustrated and angry I feel all the fucking time. That my days feel like driving our old Corvette that never got out of second without wheezing, and Harry gets the look he always gets when I talk about myself too long. Trance. But he snaps out of it when Ania asks:

'So, do you want to remain in this marriage Rose?'

'No.' Not even a millisecond of hesitation.

'Are you sure?'

'Uh, no.'

'Let me put it this way. Do you see yourself growing old with Harry?'

'Shit, I hope not.'

Then I get this shivery, quivery feeling, as if I'm shaking the last of Harry off me. The room feels oddly calm. How can it? But it does.

No it doesn't. Gone back to panicky tension again.

'This is ridiculous! No offence Ania, but these are stupid questions,' Harry suddenly says, very un-Harry-like. 'I mean, no one really knows what they want. How can they? It's not like we can travel into the future, see if we're wanting the right thing. Can't take a decision for a trial run, make sure it works out ok. We only know what we think we want. Truly.'

My god, Harry! I could kiss him! So confident and articulate! In your face, Ania!

'So basically, you're saying it's all a guessing game?' she asks, subdued.

'Yes. But with real hearts at stake.'

A killer line, but I still want to leave him. I think.

We make our next appointment with Ania and say our goodnights.

Halfway down the stairs, my heart explodes. Something is happening in my life. At last! Wait till I tell Alpin. But by the time I'm at the bottom of the stairs, my heart sinks. What have I done? What am I doing? My heart's on a trampoline, up, down, up, down. I feel nauseous. I've jettisoned all of my old Leith life, untethered myself from everything familiar, and now here I am sacking my harmless old hubby. It's scary beyond scary, yet I cannot un-say those words. They are true words and needed to be said. At least I think they're true. Fuck. If only Harry had said something stupid. Too confusing when he's clever.

In the car, he drives quicker than normal. Alpin is a fast driver, and he's clever. It's like Harry knows about him, *is becoming him,* in order to distract me.

'Fancy the pub, then?' he asks jauntily. I take a good look at his profile. Nah, he's still Harry. Rely on Harry to know how to pretend the world has not just ended. On the *Titanic*, he'd be one of those musicians playing 'Clementine', yawning as everyone else screamed and piled into lifeboats.

'Well, why not?' Though all I really want to do is log on, check my emails. 'Sam will be fine. I'll just ring him, remind him to go to bed.'

We drive back to Evanton so we can drink in The Balconie, and walk home. It occurs to me we could easily have a drink at home – cheaper and more convenient. But I don't say this. I put on a Dido CD and sing along with her, about not putting white flags above my door. It's obvious Dido has not been married. She has no idea. She'd be waving that white flag from the fucking rooftops, after a few years.

There's a fire lit in the lounge, and only a few other customers, quietly chatting in corners. Someone's playing pool in the bar next door, and the balls thwack each other, or roll, periodically.

'Wine?' asks Harry.

'Thanks. Large, red.'

He comes back with a pint and my glass.

'So!' he says. 'That was an interesting . . . uh, date with Ania. I guess that's it then.' He brushes his hands together briskly, as if brushing away our marriage. Not looking at me. Looking at the pretty barmaid as she reaches for a glass. Oh shit. He looks ok. He looks . . . younger.

'Well, I guess so,' I say. Where is my repulsion when I need it?

'And that was a bit of a waste – us moving here.'

'Don't. We're here now. We tried.'

'Well, will we keep seeing Ania, till we sort things?'

'Yeah. Good idea. We both behave better with her,' I say.

'Will we tell her?'

'Tell her what?'

'That we're splitting up,' Harry whispers.

Pause. The words are still shocking. Thrilling. Our secret.

'Nah. It seems rude to tell her. Like she'd failed. Let's leave it for a while,' I tell him, feeling swamped in my own indecisiveness. Having jumped off the damn cliff finally, can't really do the free fall. Can't let go of that safety harness just yet.

'Yeah. She's sweet really, it's not her fault.'

'We'll leave it for now.'

'No need to hurt her feelings. Nice lassie.'

Listen to us! Then we're quiet and drink, till a giggle takes hold without warning my mouth, so I spray some wine on Harry. It's the thought of us lying to Ania. Of pretending to reconcile out of politeness. Of being in cahoots, at the very brink of separation.

Harry doesn't laugh at first, just looks disgusted and wipes off his face. But then he laughs too, bless. No one else knows this about me. I'm weird as hell. It's funny when he laughs too, and I feel far more drunk than one large wine warrants.

'Fancy another?'

'Aye.'

So what do we do, after we celebrate our own demise and stumble home? We have sex. And it does not make me vomit.

Maciek

Do not think about sex with her! If I think too much about her, it will not happen. Maciek – stop rehearsing this! I shout to myself. I don't want to jinx it. Go away naked Ania pictures!

Pizza Palace is warm, and smells of garlic bread. I like it better than my caravan. I wish I could sleep here. Warm, clean, garlic air. It is a perfect place. Sam is in the back, preparing all the bases. He is a good worker. Always washes his hands, never complains.

'So, Sam, how is it with this Polish girlfriend?' I ask. I always ask him this.

'She's not my girlfriend, wanker,' he always answers. This is how we talk now. We are old friends.

'Oh well, you will need to give her a present then. Or give her a nice dinner in a nice restaurant.'

'Aye, whatever. And how's your adultery thing going?' he asks, as he slides the bases into pans.

'I am not having adultery with Ania.'

'You better get a move on,' says Sam. 'She'll be thinking you don't fancy her.'

'You are giving the piss again.'

'I am *taking* the piss.'

'So, what should I do about her?'

'Do I look like I'd know? Fuck sake Maciek, get a grip. I'm fourteen.'

'But you know her husband, you know things I do not about Ania. I can't sleep, with the thoughts I have of her.'

But Sam sighs and says: 'I hope you're just pretending to be pathetic. I don't know much, but I'm pretty sure women don't like to shag pathetic men.'

Then his work is done and his Mamusia, she takes him home. Rose is her name. A nice woman, but Sam is mean to her. He doesn't smile when she smiles, and hardly even looks at her. I do not hear him say thank you. After they go, the shop it is empty, and outside there is the sad quiet Scottish rain.

I miss the thunderstorms of Krakow. I miss the smell of them, like photocopiers. Scottish winter days are shorter than Polish. Much. And some days die before they begin. All day, no sun. I think, of course, about death at these times. You cannot study the meaning of life without death clearing his throat, like this, and saying:

Please! Don't forget me!

Every other minute, death being rude and interrupting. All those philosophers, all those words and heavy books. What does anyone really know? This:

We all die.

And perhaps this too:

Love is real.

It doesn't matter whether God, he exists or not, because it doesn't change these two facts. Everything else is just *pierogi*.

And I'll tell you what death is. It is a small, light wind, one you hardly notice, and this wind, it blows over every person on earth. Every day and especially every night. And it blows hardest on people who are loosed from their lives, and they forget to pay attention. People who are not where they belong. Or people who are in a sudden sadness. Sadness, it can disconnect you from everything. Then this wind it takes this person right off the skin of the earth. Just like that! A moment of not being careful, not looking in the rear-view mirror, and whoomph! And after a very short piece of time, it is like this person has never had a life at all. We are not big mountains. We are not big stony mountains, we are the piece of pepperoni I have just dropped on floor. See? I'm putting it in the bin. Who remembers pepperoni? Not even the other pepperonis.

I feel half here, today. Maybe I am sick. Head slow and heavy, and heart-dead. I need to remind myself: Maciek! You are seconds from being not alive! Being not dead and noticing pulls me back into my skin. And it is good to love Ania, even though she does not love me. Even though I cannot give her this love. I am alive and I love. It is enough.

I will make very good pizzas tonight, because it feels better than giving up on pizza.

Here is a family, so I smile – why not? I make talk about the weather. I make a king-sized meat feast pizza for this arguing family. They can't agree on who wins a football game. As if this is important. They are pepperoni too, but at least they are a family of pepperoni. They will notice if one of them drops to floor. They will not stand on it or toss it in the bin. Not right away.

I don't like being the only pepperoni. Everything is wrong. I miss home. My stomach hurts and my throat, it hurts too. And if Sam's right, no woman is going to love me ever again. It's been months. I will forget how to do it.

After the arguing football family leave, I phone my Ciotka, my Aunt Agata. It's very cheap to call Poland, I don't know why I don't do it more often.

'*Dzien dobry?* Maciek!' she says, and with her voice, in comes her kitchen. The terracotta tiles on the wall, the coal fire that heats four rooms at the one time. The perfume she wears. Lavender. Outside sounds too; dogs barking, cars honking, crows. I feel something, it pours into me. All my growing up is there. Ciotka's voice gives me back to myself.

'Maciek?' says my good Ciotka.

I reach for my answer, and at first I have no Polish words, just this sore throat. A tiny piece of time, but it makes my heart flump. Then I'm back. The words are liquid, and Pizza Palace is nowhere.

'*Dzien dobry!*' I say, growing large. Have you ever noticed how happiness makes you grow large inside?

She asks how I am, and how this place is, and then she says: 'Tak, tak, tak,' like she always does, and asks:

'When are you coming home? You come for Christmas, yes?'

And I say, because money doesn't matter sometimes: 'Yes, I'll come home for Christmas. I'll be home.'

'Do you promise this, Maciek Kowalczyk? To come home for Christmas?'

'Yes. Yes!'

She says that she misses me, that she loves me, and it is like she is saying *have a nice day*, like a thing you say to everyone when it is time for hanging up. Or a thing that is so constantly true, it does not need a special voice or time to say it. I cannot tell the difference, so I say it too – quick, like her – 'I love you. I miss you! See you next month.' Then I hang up.

For a few minutes Poland comes to shore then, and it is Pizza Palace that the tide washes away. All the sad sour feelings, all the good sweet things, of home. Agata. Marja. And somehow, Mamusia too. She dies, but she is still there. Poland takes up space in my chest. Right here.

In comes an ugly woman, and she says something.

'What? Please, can you please tell me again? What do you want?'

This ugly woman with her ugly mouth open, shows all her ugly yellow teeth; I cannot understand what she says. Just noise, no meaning. Pizza, I tell myself. She must be saying pizza words, listen to her Maciek! But it is like the first day in Scotland again. My mind is full of thick black clouds, and I cannot speak, and cannot get warm, and no one looks like a friend. Scottish people are not how I thought they'd be. They are not *uprzejmy*. The ugly woman, she looks angry now. There is spit on her chin, and she smells like egg.

But my life, it is saved!!! Behind this angry, ugly woman is suddenly Ania.

This is big. This is very big.

I have to go around counter, past the noisy, ugly woman, and I put my arms around Ania. At first she does not move. She thinks I am crazy. How can she know what day I am in? The death thoughts, the homesickness? I am crazy. I hold tighter, and then I feel her shake, like she is laughing. Then her arms, they are around me too.

Ugly woman leaves, and says: 'Fuck you, then.'

'Fuck you very much too,' I say back to her, over Ania's most beautiful in the world head.

Sam

Puke. My parents are fucking at it.

There they are, snogging at the kitchen sink. His hand is up her top. Tossers.

'Yous two are disgusting,' I tell them. They freeze, then giggle, and I march out of the room. Slam the door hard. I hate them.

On the way to school, I'm thinking the obvious solution: Run away.

Just take favourite things.

iPod

Phone

Money from Mum's bag (she never notices)

Newest jeans and tops

Trainers

It'll all fit in one bag. I'll sneak out before they get home from work. Where will I go?

Need a place with a bed. And a place to recharge the iPod and phone. So, a bed and electricity. And food, so a kitchen to make food in, which I can do myself no bother. There's Gran's house down in Leith. Nah, she'd only ring Mum, and that'd be that.

Where, where, where can I go?

Maciek's caravan!!!

This is genius. *I* am genius. Maciek lives alone, he'd not mind. And could even see the folks from time to time.

Him and me, we get on fine, like. I can sleep on the sofa bit that folds down.

He doesn't talk much, but talking's crap anyway. Only fags talk.

When I get off the bus at school, I've totally left home already. Life is good. I've even got this new walk. Like I'm older. Cooler. I don't take any shit from anyone. Do I miss Mum and Dad? My old bedroom? Hmmmmm . . . nope! Don't miss any of it. This must be what life'll be, what being an adult's like. Sound. Bring it on. Families suck.

In maths class, I sit right down next to her, and as if I've always done this, say:

'*Dobranoc stolik!*'

She smiles. 'No, Sam. It is morning, not night. And I am not a table. But your accent, it is very good. I did not know you spoke Polish. *Dzien dobry!*'

I'm feeling thick now, but I can't stop. I say:

'*Prosze mi to pokazac na planie jablko?*'

'Sam, this is good! Very good!'

'Do you know what I said?'

'Not a word! But this is not being the important thing.'

Roksana does not smile much. But she is smiling now, like you would not believe.

This smile seems to spread out so that later, her smile is everywhere I look.

Ania

Now he is everywhere. This man, this tall double-lidded stranger from the country of my father. It's not so much that I notice him now, at the swimming pool or Pizza Palace or Tesco café. It's more that I notice when he is not there. If I look where he should be and he is not, I experience an ache in my chest and also I feel little breathless, as if my heart is being both squeezed and slackened. Then there is this rising feeling in my throat. And if I have not seen him for a few days, there is a gathering weight in my chest, till I feel quite edgy and impatient. As if his absence results in an actual substance filling me up. It is all very fascinating. And disturbing.

But does it mean anything? These are just the physical manifestations of expectations not met. Normally, when I am able to analyse emotion, I can put it away. And so I shouldn't be disappointed and disturbed when a day goes by and I don't see Maciek. Awareness should cancel out, not emotion, but ambushes of emotion. I have a degree in dealing with the effects of Macieks.

I love my marriage and I want a baby. Tonight when I cook tea for Ian, I will light some candles and play that Amy Winehouse CD he bought a few weeks ago. Not my cup of tea, but he likes it. I'll wear my red top with the lacy trim, and spray myself with Chanel. I'll open the bottle of pricey wine Dad gave us last Hogmanay. Almost a whole year and we've had no cause to open it! But an occasion can be special because one decides to make it special. A dinner can be romantic because one knows all the ingredients of a romantic dinner, and uses them. I am empty, flat, contemplating all this intimacy and romance, but isn't that the whole purpose of ritual? To give us a framework to fill in? The appearance of normality can summon normality. Physician, heal thyself!

But then – oh no! He comes home early, catches me off guard. Still in my baggiest jeans, dinner half cooked, candles unlit, perfume-less.

'How was work?' I ask.

'Hell,' he says as usual. He opens a beer. 'How was your day? Save any marriages?'

'Maybe. I hope so.' Ian always remembers to ask about my job. The fact it is very part-time, and practically unpaid never comes into it. 'I opened that nice bottle, by the way.'

'What bottle?'

'This bottle. The one my dad gave us ages ago.'

'We've still got that? What on earth for?'

'It's expensive. I wanted to save it.'

'So why are you wanting to drink it now?' he asks, quite logically, while looking through the post. His logic was one of the reasons I married him.

'I thought we could . . .'

'Could what?'

'Drink it anyway,' I say weakly, basting the roast pork, which all of a sudden seems not that special a meal. We have roast pork almost weekly.

'Good enough! Carry on. I'm on beer, myself,' he announces, as he leaves the kitchen on his way to a shower, neglecting to plant his customary kiss on my cheek. And he doesn't usually fling his jacket down on the sofa like that, does he?

Ian is the father of all the children I will have. He is the most important person in my life, and I know him as well as I know myself. Nothing he could do or say should surprise me. But unease ripples through me, I feel quite queasy from it. I make myself sit down and breathe slowly, and remind myself that this is normal. This is what a marriage is sometimes. Not always feeling like you know your partner.

I set the table carefully, pour myself a glass of wine. I have never been drunk – you don't believe me? I don't understand why anyone would want to lose control. I quite enjoy the taste, but never the effect. I put on the Amy Winehouse CD. I don't change my clothes or put on perfume, but at the last moment, as if it means nothing really, I light all the candles till the kitchen is transformed into a cosy and mysterious place. Where better to meet a stranger? But the wine tastes terrible, and I can't finish my glass. And I hardly touch my food.

Next afternoon, I'm in Dingwall and am suddenly starving, too hungry to even wait till I get home. No appetite for breakfast at all earlier. I want something greasy and stodgy, right now. I want pizza. Maciek is there, but before I can even say hello or smile, which I fully intend to do, he flings himself at me, wraps his enormous arms around me. How dare he! I wait for him to stop and when he doesn't, I tell my arms to push him away. This is wrong. An emergency alarm has been set off, with a tinny voice in my head screaming: Detach! Danger, danger! Detach! But then the voice is suddenly . . . shut down, mid-syllable. And for the first time in my life while awake, I stop having thoughts. My brain is sedated. But my muscles and blood seem to have a wisdom of their own, and are not sedated.

It feels exactly like falling, and my arms go round him so I won't hit the ground.

Weirdly clichéd, the whole experience. What can I say? It's like discovering Santa Claus really does exist.

Rose

What can I say? Lust is a bugger. Machine-guns defences to smithereens.

Got a mind of its own entirely, and doesn't bother explaining itself. Or apologising. Actually, everything these days seems to have a mind of its own, except my own fucking mind. I am so lust-sensitised now, I only have to see Alpin's name in my inbox to get wet.

Do you miss me?

I miss you.

How much?

I can't sleep.

What do you want?

I want you.

I want to want Harry. Life would be so much easier if I did. I've tried closing my eyes and pretending he's someone else. Alpin even, though that always feels so ridiculous, I end up giggling. I've tried getting very drunk, in fact I think this has driven me to wino-ism. Haven't tried porn, thongs, or sex therapy. But I've tried telling myself he'll not be part of my life much longer. I tell myself: It's safe to give Harry all you can, he'll be gone tomorrow! But no. It's evaporated, that horniness after our last session with Ania. And our marriage rolls on, oblivious to our conversations about splitting up. Each night I crawl into bed with Harry, curl up away from him and sigh. Each night marks the end of another day of my decreasing life. I am chickening out. Then another night comes, and another morning. And before I know it, like obedient children, we arrive punctually at Ania's apricot-jam room again.

'How is the marriage going? Harry?' she asks with her usual professional warmth. Except there's something not quite the same, and now I think of it, she was a bit off last time too. Something has ruffled her smoothness.

'Better in some ways, but not great,' says Harry.

'I'm glad to hear you say that, Harry. These things can take a long time, and need to be worked at. Just remember that a better marriage is possible. An important attitude. Realistic yet positive. Rose? How are you?'

'Great!' I lie robustly.

Ania's eyebrows rise, like she's totally not buying it. So I say:

'I think it's all down to standards. To expectations. Harry has higher expectations than me. He always has done.'

'What was your parents' marriage like, Harry?' asks Ania.

They've both been dead for years, and Harry never talks about them.

'Mum and Dad? I don't know. They always seemed to just get on with things. Don't remember any fights at all. Not a lot of roses and wine either, but then who knows what really went on. I think they were probably quite happy with each other. You know. Liked each other.'

'And how about your parents, Rose. What was their marriage like?'

'Hell. They should have split up. Constant bickering. Constant rows and doors slamming and accusations. Competitive! I think they're jealous of each other, all the time. Each thinking the other's getting a better deal.'

'But they didn't part?'

'Nah. They're still together. Some days I think they love hating each other. Honestly. There is something almost gleeful in their arguing. Like a battle they're addicted to. And more. Proud of.'

I feel a bit proud of them too, thinking of their spectacular rows. Such energy!

'Interesting.'

'Why, anyway? What's their marriage got to do with anything? I've done my best not to marry someone like my dear old dad, not repeat the pattern. But here we are.'

Ania doesn't say anything for a few seconds. She has this annoying habit of making people wait for her to arrange her words.

'Often, I think we are drawn, not to the right person – someone who would bring out our best qualities – but to situations we're familiar with. It's not so much that we are happy or unhappy. More to do with feeling comfortable. At home in a relationship.'

'Well, I'm not at home in this one,' says Harry. 'She's driving me crazy. Always has done.'

'You mean from the start? When you first knew each other?'

'Aye.'

'And how did you two begin? What was the courtship like?'

Courtship? Are we in *Pride and Prejudice* land? We just look at her blankly.

'Well, how about the wedding?'

'Disaster,' we say in unison. Then we both open our mouths again, as if to say more, then close them. And there's that little worm of a giggle, again, wanting out. Harry makes me laugh. I don't understand how someone I do not respect or fancy, someone who irritates me intensely, can still have this effect.

Then Ania goes on her high horse again:

'Perhaps how a marriage begins is not terribly important. It is brave and difficult, just to begin a life with someone. Not a single person knows whom they are marrying, really. Newlyweds are all novices, stumbling in the dark. It's like becoming a parent for the first time.'

And then I spot it – Ania's hand slipping over her belly. Her boobs are bigger, I swear. And she's got that look. Like she's stoned. She's totally up the spout!

'Or for the second or third or fourth time for that matter. Even second or third or fourth marriages are entered into by totally inexperienced people. What you learn on one person, you cannot just apply to another.'

Harry is drifting off, I can tell by his attentive pose. Like he cares.

'And weddings – they're completely separate from marriage. They don't give you anything you need for a good marriage.'

Well, duh.

Ania pauses, leans forward, cleavage peeking. Harry snaps to and leans forward too.

'Everybody thinks they know the person they marry,' says Ania. 'And they're all wrong! Especially they can't know who that person will become in ten years, in thirty-five years. How can they? Their spouse will be someone else, and so will they. A long marriage is a process of constantly re-acquainting yourself with the person you eat breakfast with. People marry a series of strangers they have not met yet.'

Ok. Whatever. I actually have a lot I want to say tonight. I've been rehearsing. If Ania keeps up this lecture about marriage, I'll forget my lines.

'Everyone knows the statistics of divorce,' continues Ania. 'And they know about all the miserable marriages that don't end in divorce. And all the so-so marriages, too mediocre to warrant celebration or divorce.'

Like the vast majority, I want to say.

'At the point of marrying, nobody believes divorce will happen to them. Did you?'

'Well, no,' says Harry.

'Sure. It wasn't going to happen to us,' I scoff.

'Getting married is one of the greatest leaps of faith human beings are capable of,' says Ania in her wise voice.

Oh, get over yourself.

I say: 'But no courage at all is really required, if you think your marriage will be different. That's how we were, anyway. Not brave. Cocky. And hungover.'

'You may have been idealistic Rose, but you were brave nonetheless. To forfeit all other romantic adventures for one man.'

'Nah. Truly, I never thought like that. I never said to myself: you will never, ever, kiss another man as long as you live.'

'Well, there goes that illusion,' sighs Harry.

'Sorry, but I am not that deep. I was thinking about having a family, and you wanted to get married, and it seemed a good enough offer, a good enough time. I was tired of being on my own.'

'So I was, like, the guy who happened to be there? The soft landing.'

'Oh stop. As if it wasn't the same for you. Marriage is totally a bolthole. The perfect place to hide from . . .'

'Intimacy?' offers Ania. 'Well, there may be some truth in that. Ironically, marriage can be the perfect excuse to not engage with people, but not many people would admit that as a motive. A spouse can shield you from all sorts of things. But what happened at the beginning, to make you want to marry each other? Can you both remember the beginning?'

'As in a nice way?' I ask.

'I blame drink,' says Harry.

'Ditto,' I say. 'It began with a lousy mood and some gin and tonics. Fancied Harry after the fifth.'

'The Boat and Paddle, Tony's wedding. Totally sozzled.'

We cackle, me and Harry, like dirty old men. Ania just stares, with this dippy polite smile.

'Now come on, you two,' scolds Ania. 'Be serious for a minute. Let's go back.'

So, chastened, we sit quiet a minute. Then into the quiet, to my utter astonishment, Harry says:

'To be honest, I couldn't believe my luck.'

He speaks directly to Ania, as if I'm not here.

'Rose, now she was way out of my league. But I was pissed, and I told her she looked familiar, and asked if we'd met before. She said I looked familiar too. Then she said: Have I slept with you?'

Ania doesn't react of course, she has zero sense of humour. And I already know this story, so I'm mute, and after a second Harry continues.

'Very suspicious, when she agreed to go out with me. I'd only asked her out as kind of a joke, never thought she'd say: Aye, alright then. She was one of the pretty girls who went out all the time. When she said aye, I had to rethink that. Maybe she wasn't so cool, I mean. But I didn't hold it against her for very long. Her liking me.'

'Do you mean you thought less of her, for liking you?'

'In a way. I mean, she could've had anyone. If she'd been who I thought she was, she would have done much better than me.'

Fuck off Harry, I think. No way. But he's still not looking at me. Is he blushing? Hell. Ania must be eating this up.

'What made you love Rose?'

'Love her? I fancied the pants off her, tell you the truth. Don't know about love. All my mates were getting married, and that. Seemed the right thing to do. Right time.'

Harry crosses his legs, stretches his fingers.

'So you proposed? How long had you known her?'

'Oh ages. At least six months.'

'And?'

'And, so, one night when we were, you know, at it. Well, she actually passed out after, and looked kind of . . . well, she looked a bit daft. Silly, I know, but she didn't look her prettiest. Her chin had kind of doubled up, and her mouth was hanging open with wee bit drool sliding out of it, and . . .'

Now it's me blushing. I so do not need this.

'And?'

'Well, and I thought to myself, if I can still fancy her looking like this, she'll do for me.'

'So, you convinced yourself you were seeing her as unattractive as she could be, so it was a good way to measure your love?'

'Well, don't know if I really thought about it that way, but what happened was I whispered to her while she was passed out. I said: So, what do you say, will we tie the bloody knot and have done with it?'

'You proposed to her when she was unconscious?'

This is good. I love this bit.

'Well, just to kind of try it out, like. See how the words felt out loud, near her.'

'And?'

'And would you believe it, she actually opened her eyes and said: Aye, alright then.'

'So she was listening?'

'Must have been. Must have been a fake sleep. A fake pass-out to trick me.'

Now that is just paranoid. I was lying still because if I moved, I might've puked.

'And she held you to it the next day?'

'Damn right she did. Next thing I knew, her mum and dad were calling me Son. As in, would you like to stop for your tea, Son? Steak alright with you? All her pals started winking at me, and their fellas started slapping me on the back, and buying me pints.'

'And this was good? It felt right?'

'It was, well, it was what it was. It felt funny, but alright. I mean, nearly all my mates had already done it, and I figured it must be ok. Be the right thing. I was almost twenty-four.'

'I see,' says Ania, in her considering non-judgemental way. Then she turns to me.

'Rose? How about you? Do you remember falling in love with Harry?'

I giggle and instantly despise myself.

'Sorry. It's just me and Harry – we don't do love. Or the mush stuff.' But me and Alpin do. When he first told me he loved me, I gave him the best blow job of my life. And maybe his too.

Ania looks at me coolly and waits. Sure she was more friendly with Harry.

'Alright. It's true, what he's saying – all our friends were getting married. And also true that I felt, well, above him in some ways. But only in the way most women feel about men. He seemed so . . . so simple. I don't know. I just felt like I was quicker than him, and saw more in people.'

'And you fell in love with his . . . ?'

'Ok, this is what I remember. It was near the beginning, and I'd been without a boyfriend for about six months at that time. Been seeing quite a few guys, but none of them hitting the mark.'

'They'd all dumped her,' says Harry.

'One of them! Only one dumped me!'

'Harry, let Rose speak.'

'Sorry.'

'So, there I was, about twenty-five, feeling a little bit, to be honest, a bit desperate, and it was a horrible day.'

'What day?'

'This day I am trying to tell you about. It was dark and wet and depressing, and I'd had a horrible haircut, and my shoes were wet, and so were my socks. I was sitting in the café and I was waiting.'

'I think I remember,' says Harry. 'Was it that time I was meeting you to do some Christmas shopping? That was how much I fancied you – even let you take me round the shops.'

'Not that you've ever done it since.'

'Like you need some help spending money.'

'Now, now,' says Ania. 'Let's stick to the point. Rose, you were telling us about waiting for Harry at the café on a horrible day.'

'Yes. Well, I don't know why I always remember this.' And I do. It's downright weird. 'Harry was late, and I was worried that he wasn't coming. That he'd sussed what a moody cow I was. But I knew he was coming, really. Deep down, I knew. I sat there and looked around at all the other shoppers, and I remember telling myself: The day is crap, my job is crap, my haircut is crap. But here I am, waiting for my boyfriend! And this gave me such a thrill, I repeated it, over and over to myself. My boyfriend is coming to meet me. And then, there he was.'

'And that is when you fell in love with Harry? When you finally saw him coming towards you?'

I stall for time by re-crossing my legs and then coughing.

I gear myself for saying: Yes! That's when I knew I was in love!

But a series of sneezes mysteriously queue up behind my sinuses, and I have to turn away and apologise before expelling them into my hand.

And between the second and third sneeze, I am reminded that I have never fallen in love with Harry.

'I loved saying my boyfriend. And later, I loved saying my husband.'

'Great,' snorts Harry.

'Well, if you hadn't met me, do you imagine you would be single now? Did you really imagine I was the only woman on earth you could've married?'

Harry looks disgusted. 'Oh Harry. We didn't have a clue. We were never right for each other.'

Silence.

'Perhaps it hardly matters,' says Ania, in that tone, 'if you choose the right person. Sometimes marriage can make the other person the right person, just by being the wife or husband. Maybe just getting up every day with the same person makes them the right person. Harry, don't you feel you've changed over the years to accommodate Rose? And I am sure she has altered too. We all affect the people we are close to, and if the marriage is a success, we become a better person as a result. So it hardly matters if you marry for the right reasons, or that you marry the right person – being with them can make them the right person.'

So we sit like two lumps and stare at her. Frozen by a mutual reluctance to let her reassure us.

'But we weren't in love, not really. Never. And we don't even have a song,' I say, detesting the whine in my voice.

'And besides,' joins Harry loyally, 'Rose isn't even remotely my type.'

Ania thinks about this for a moment, then says:

'All marriages are like journeys, and all journeys begin badly.'

So this is still the beginning? One helluva long start.

'Well, that is the theory anyway,' Ania says, sounding less than her usual certain self, resulting in me suddenly liking her a bit. 'And that is the end of our time tonight.'

Hoo-fucking-ray.

DECEMBER

Evanton

Even a place as small as Evanton has a place for everyone. There is Swordale Road for hill people, who need views, and there are places like Camden and Livera Streets for people who crave snugness. There are all the scattered farm cottages and farmhouses on the outskirts, for people who like to feel space around them. There are modern central-heated bungalows for those who like newness, and old stone houses for people who think the charm of history outweighs draughty rooms. Socially, incomers tend to make friends with other incomers, and locals cluster with other locals, but they all choose houses based on their inclinations, not origin. Every street has a mixture of locals and incomers.

The people in Evanton who are in the wrong place are puzzled by their own restlessness, and often re-arrange furniture or change their wallpaper, to no avail.

Rose and Harry are living on the right street, cosily in a terrace in the heart of Evanton. Ania is happy in her bungalow on Swordale Road, but Ian would be happier lower down. By contrast, Sam finds his house too dark and low. Maciek would be happiest in one of the outlying cottages, but only if he found someone to live with.

The community council – mostly Camden and Livera Street people – have organised a Christmas tree lighting. The tree has been donated by the local estate, and stands asymmetrically, by the car park across from the pub. This is a village without a square, but they make do. Of course the lights do not go on immediately after the countdown – even the youngest Evantonians look stoically on, with rain dripping down their wind whipped faces, while someone – a hill person – tackles the generator. Finally the lights are lit, and the tree, which was so ordinary a second ago, so ludicrous and lopsided, is not.

It is 5:30. The sun set an hour ago.

Maciek

And worse thing of all: Everywhere, Christmas. Santa Claus and holly and bells, hanging by wires between lampposts. And these songs, all the time in every shop and on the radio. And where is the snow? No snow. Sam agrees it is terrible. He wants snow too. We sit in my caravan, bored with rain. Sam comes here a lot now, almost every day after school, for a little while. Half an hour. We fart and burp with each other; this means we're old friends already. We talk about rain, often, because it is always raining.

'I've got a new snowboard I've only used twice. Total bitch, this rain.'

'Please, Sam, this rain is no good, but it's a not girl dog. And not a bad woman either. It is rain, that is all.'

'Eh? Bitch is anything I'm a bit fed up with, Maciek.'

'Alright, thank you,' I say, because I like to know these things. Sam is funny, and not like talking to a kid at all. More like talking to a grownup, who hasn't done much yet.

'Sam, do you want to learn some more words in Polish?'

'Go on then, bitch.'

'I am not a bitch, Sam. I am your friend.'

'I know Maciek. That was bitch in a friendly way. I meant it to be funny.'

'I am your bitch friend?'

'Too far, Maciek. Too far.'

I think I will not in a million years understand English.

In Poland, there's been snow for four weeks now. Yesterday I phone my Ciotka again, and she says everything is white there, and beautiful. She says she has made a room ready for me, with new duvet and matching curtains. And Christmas will be a family party. I belong home, she tells me.

'When are you moving back home?'

'I don't know. But I'll see you at Christmas. A few weeks.'

'You should be here, not in Scotland, Maciek. Marja was not worth moving away for.'

'How do you know that is why I left?'

'Everyone is knowing that, Maciek. What, you think your eyes say nothing?'

'I like Scotland. It is a good place.'

'Come home Maciek. We are a good place too. Better to be home.'

A day seems to last only a few hours, then it's dark again. And cold. It is cold inside my blood. And of course, you know what happens when you feel the world is a cold place, and you don't know where your home is, and the woman you love has a husband? A man, he will come to you and say a mean thing right in front of your face.

Yes.

Tonight after Sam has gone, I'm in the pub, where I sit by the fire and drink beer. I hear him. I don't know his name, just someone who is here many times. He can't see my face because of my hat. I hear him say to his friends: 'They fookin' take all the jobs and then send the bloody money home. I tell you, we're being fleeced. Scotland's had it, if this keeps up. They're fookin' everywhere now.'

Then one of his friends, he tells a story about a restaurant, and the waitress is a Polish woman, and she doesn't understand what he asks for. She brings him the wrong food. The wrong drink. Gives him the wrong money. And his own wife, she can't get a job in this restaurant. This makes all the men nod their stupid heads, and they say in stupid voices: 'Aye. Not right. Not right at fookin' all.'

Then I want to go home, because I know. I know what they talk about. I'm almost at the caravan park, when I hear the footsteps, and this man he suddenly walks faster than me and he says, just when he's passing me:

'Fooking Pole. Fook off back home, cunt.'

That is all. Then he walks past me, and my heart is beating fast, and I hear my voice:

'No! *You* fuck off! You stupid . . . you stupid bitch!'

The man, he turns around and I think – *Oh kurwa!* What did I shout?

He looks like he's reaching for something in his pocket and I almost piss myself. I am a weak man, I have almost no muscles, look! But I stand very tall, and I shout: '*Kurwa mac!*'

Which is the rudest way of saying fuck you. I say it like an angry dog, with my throat. I can't believe I can be this way. But it works. He spits at me but walks away, fast.

Run fast, bitch man. I am a lion!

It is so dark, and I'm home. But it is not. It is not a home.

And inside, I see my bread is furry now. I boil the kettle for tea, but there are no tea bags. And the rain, while I was out, it found an open place in the roof, and now my bed is wet. Even the rain stinks tonight. It smells like the old men who sit all day in the park at home. Then I empty my pockets and cannot find my wallet.

These are some of the things that happen when it rains instead of snows, and you love Snow White but she has a husband.

The next morning is not a workday, and I find my wallet in my other pocket. I am in the co-op. This is to buy my breakfast. Bacon and eggs, a bag of French rolls. And I can feel that she is in the shop with me. There she is. In the queue. First time, since the hug. She is very *seksowny* and I am hard just seeing her. Forget the eggs and bacon, I stand behind her with just my rolls.

But she looks very cold. And ill.

'Ania,' I say. 'Are you alright?'

'Hello Maciek,' she says. My name in her voice! She is saying she loves me, just by saying my name. Stupid. I know what you think. Laugh at me, go on. Poor pathetic Maciek, who is happy for such a small reason.

'Yes, I'm fine,' she says. 'Do I look sick? It's this time of year. No, actually, you're right. I do feel a bit sick.' Then she turns away and says quietly, maybe to herself only: 'I must be sick.'

I have thought many times about our hug. Many times of this. Exactly what happens is this: I hold her and she does not at first move. Then she puts her arms this way, around my middle, and her head falls here, below my chin. She makes a sad noise with no words. And then, this is the part I keep going back to. She pulls me close. I almost lose Pizza Palace then, my heart it explodes. I think – what now? A kiss? But before I can kiss her, she lets go, and then she is gone. Without a pizza.

Now we are in the co-op. There is one man in the queue before her, and he is almost finished. There is little time.

'Ania, how sick? It is the flu? Are you sick in your stomach? Headache?'

She does not say any words for a minute, even though she is looking right at me. As I watch her face, it loses all colour.

'My stomach,' she says. 'And I feel faint.'

It is her turn now, and she gives to the shop girl a DVD, a loaf of bread and a newspaper. The shop girl pings the till and Ania pays her. I think hard, fast, what to say to keep her here, but suddenly she is finished and says:

'Nice to see you, Maciek.'

And out the door she does go.

I pay for my rolls, not even look at the change. I leave the shop, and think that is it. But miracle! She sits on the bench outside. She is leaning over, with her head in her hands.

'Ania, please. What is wrong? I can walk you home, and I'll take your bag. It's not a problem.'

'Oh! That is so kind of you, Maciek. But I think I just need to sit here a moment.'

'Do you live far from here?'

'No, just up the road a bit. Swordale Road.'

'Ah.' I know this already, of course.

'I don't know what's wrong with me. I just feel so weak. So tired.'

'Perhaps you work too hard. What is your work?'

'I'm a marriage counsellor. It can be very tiring, but it's a good job.'

'You tell married people how to save their marriage, yes?'

'Mostly I just listen to them talk about why they're unhappy.'

'Is marriage a thing worth saving?'

She thinks for a minute. I can see her thinking. This is a person who is careful when she speaks.

'A good marriage is. A good marriage can save a life.'

I have to stop myself from embracing her, this freezing woman I don't even know the last name of.

'You must know a lot about love,' I say.

'Hmm . . . I *think* about it a lot.'

'Me too. I'm philosopher, you know.'

She smiles a little at this, as if I've made a joke.

'I mean my degree, it is in philosophy. In Krakow, I teach at the college.'

'Oh. I figured you weren't the typical Pizza Palace man.'

'Ah, but who is he? Everybody thinks and feels his own way.'

'Aye, of course. It was a careless thing to say. A snobby thing.'

'Not at all. It is how we all think. There is not enough time, otherwise.'

'I suppose not.'

'I think, perhaps, we are both philosophers.'

'Perhaps. Perhaps.'

I sit as close as I can without touching her. Her hands, white and small, are on her lap, and they must be cold. Where are her gloves?

'Why are you called Ania? Did you know it's Polish name?'

'Aye. My father's Polish. My maiden name is Zamoyski.'

'From where?'

'From Kalisz.'

'Ah.'

'Have you been there?'

'No. But I know where it is. A nice place, I think. Small. Farms.'

'I'd love to go one day.' But she doesn't sound excited. She yawns and shivers at same time. I watch this shudder, it goes through her top to bottom.

'Do you know what we do in Poland, Ania, when there's a day like this, and we are very cold and tired?'

Ania closes her eyes a moment. Her eyelids show capillaries. Her skin is so thin.

'What do you do?' she whispers.

'We boil a kettle and make tea,' I say.

She opens her eyes, with a disappointed look.

'And we do not add milk. We add some raspberry . . . squash, you would call it.'

Ania's face squishes up, like this is not a good picture.

'And if it is a very, very cold and miserable day, and nothing is right, and we have perhaps a very bad cough, then we sometimes open a small bottle of Gold Wasser.'

She stares at me. What eyes! I will not tell you words like blue and lovely. But think of the last time you were in love. Think of electricity.

'My Ciotka, she keeps a bottle in the cupboard, up high.'

'Gold what?'

'Gold Wasser.'

I know when quiet is good, and I stop talking and let her make her own picture. She sits better now, not bent over. Her face is pink.

'What is it?' she asks, so soft I have to watch her lips.

It's like when she says my name – this whisper on the shop

bench. There is no one else in Evanton but us. Such an elephant compliment, this whisper says to me.

'Ania.' I love saying her name. 'Ania.'

'Yes?'

'It is hard to explain. Gold Wasser is clear, like water, and there is gold floating in it.'

'Not real gold?'

'Yes. Real gold.'

'How can you drink it?'

'They are small slivers, like shavings.'

'Invisible?'

'No. You can see them in bottle. But they are easy to swallow.'

'And the water full of gold – what does it taste like?'

'It is not water, it is spirit. Very strong. And it taste like . . . roses. And like cinnamon and ginger. Like sun in middle of winter. Like a piece of spicy sugar cane.' Like the end of all sorrows, I want to say.

Ania's pupils, they grow big. Her eyes are so light, it is easy to watch her pupils. She cannot hide anything, with eyes so blue-white and her pupils getting bigger for everyone to see.

'We can't buy it here, can we?'

'There is Gold Wasser here, but is not the same. Not as strong. Not legal in this country to sell so much alcohol in one bottle. But always I have some. I bring it from Krakow.'

'Are you going home for Christmas?'

'Yes. Next week.'

'Good. Good to be home for Christmas.'

'And I'll bring back some more Gold Wasser.'

'It sounds like an elixir,' she whispers again, like I am her only friend, and she wishes to stay all day on this cold bench.

'I know this word. *Eliksir* is Polish word,' I whisper back in our private tent. '*Eliksir* . . . is like a magic medicine, yes?'

'Aye. A delicious tonic that cures everything, maybe even stops death. That can change base metals into gold.'

'Ah. Gold Wasser cannot do all these things.'

'But you said it has real gold flakes in it. Gold that can be swallowed. Gold that can make you drunk.'

And then, as if we have been talking about it all along, she asks: 'Do you believe in life after death?'

And I think to myself that this is the beginning. We will be friends now, and talk all the time about life and death and love, and we will understand each other. Me and Ania, this Scottish woman with Polish name, who is so pale she is almost transparent.

But I am wrong. We will not be friends.

I take Ania's small, cold white hands, and her bag, and I know what to do. We walk to the caravan park. Not a word we speak. When we are near my caravan, I let an arm go around her and pull her to my side, like this. She fits fine. And she has a sigh.

She says she has a husband. I say that is fine, even though I think it is, well it is unfortunate.

Inside, I unbutton her coat and she moves her arms like this, so I can take it off. She shivers, even though I left the heater on and the caravan is warm. So I hold her. She doesn't hold me, but that is fine. I try to lift her face to kiss, and she almost lets me. Then her face, it is against my shirt again.

'Shhh,' I say to her. 'Shush.'

And I sit her on the sofa. Take off her shoes and put them in front of heater. Then I take off my own coat and pour two Gold Wassers. It is so quiet. Not even a dog barking. There is a sound in my ears. It is my heart rushing. I give Ania a glass, and hope it is a clean glass but I see that she is not looking. She drinks and coughs a little.

'*Na zdrowie!*' I say.

She smiles then, and says: 'Cheers!' But it is not a real smile. How is it possible that I know this, when I don't know her?

She drinks the whole glass, fast, and says:

'Thank you, Maciek. You are kind.' She stands up. 'I'd better go now.' But she just stands there, so I pull her jumper off, over her head. Slowly unbutton her blouse, and take that off too.

Under, she wears a white top, and I push this up, and her bra, and I put both my hands over her breasts. I just rest them there. There is not sex in this, and she lets me. Then I move my hands down on both sides of her middle. I hold her hips, feel the bones. Outside, some noise finally. The Inverness train. A car honking. I undo her belt. She is quiet and not moving. But with me, I think. When she opens her mouth to breathe, I slip my hand into her underpants, and slide this finger deep up inside her.

I want to marry Ania. She is the one. We will marry! I begin this thought, before she leaves. We will live in a nice cottage, outside the village, and have chickens. Or in Inverness, maybe. In a house by the river, so we can hear the water, always. Not here. Not in a caravan in the middle of the village. How many children? I think, maybe just one, so we have lots of time alone.

Sam

We're alone in the caravan, and I finally get round to asking him, but:

'Sorry,' says Maciek.

'How not?' I ask. 'I'll no make a mess, and I can give you some money and all.'

'Sam, I do not want this money. Your parents, they are very sad to even know you talk like this.'

'How do you know?'

'I see they are nice people just by looking at you, Sam. Look at you! You are a nice boy. Healthy. Polite. It is easy for me to see this. You are only angry at them for some reason. No reason to run away.'

'You don't get it. Sure, they act nice all the time. People don't know. My mum, she cheated on my dad. My dad acts like it never happened. And they drive me insane – always wanting to know how I am, in that pointless way. Like they'd understand anything at all in my life. Like they'd actually do anything I asked. Maciek, if you met them, you'd know right away. They're freaks. They're screwing with me.'

'Screwing? Listen to me, Sam. I understand parents can be . . . very annoying sometimes.'

'So, that's a definite no, then. You think I should stay with them?'

'Yes. You come here anytime, for cup of tea, a piece of cake. You are lucky.'

'Yeah, you probably don't have dumbass parents.'

So Maciek tells me about his mum being dead, and about the dad no one knows anything about. He's no parents. Lucky bastard.

But you've got to feel sorry for him. Wonder if he's taking any presents home to Poland next week. Like batch tartan teddies and shortbread and malt whisky. Maybe some normal food, like bread and tins of beans. Poland's poor. A wee place, much smaller than Britain, with no sea. Not sure exactly where it is – somewhere to the right of Spain I think – but I know it's poor.

I know what! I'll give Maciek a Christmas prezzie. A good one, maybe the best one he'll get. I don't know what, but something amazing. A shirt maybe.

'So Maciek, what size are you?'

'This size you are seeing.'

'Extra large, then.'

I already got a prezzie for Roksana. A pair of dolphin earrings. In a tidy wooden box you can use for other stuff. I can already see them on her.

Then, and this proves Maciek is psychic, he says:

'Sam, you are in love with this Polish girl, yes?'

'What if I am?'

'That is a good thing. Don't look at me that way, like I called you bad name. I think in love, it is . . . it is a crazy thing, yes? Scary and makes you crazy, but Sam . . .'

'What?' Not sure I want to hear. Bordering on over-share. I want to tell him I am way too young to be in love, but we both know it's a lie.

'It is exciting, no? It does not happen every day. It is the most exciting thing there is.'

Then he stops and frowns. Obviously still hung up on Mrs MacLeod, then. 'It can make us do things we would never do. It makes us into different people. Every atom, different.'

'Every electron and proton and nucleus of every atom?' I have to take it this far, because we've just done that in science class and I am, above all, a smart-ass.

'Oh yes. Fall in love does this Sam. Watch out! You think you know who you are, and what your life is. Fall in love laughs at that.'

Well, that explains a lot. Not. All I want is to pull her, and hopefully, at some point in the next ten years, stop thinking about her.

Ania

I wish I could stop thinking. I wish I could sleep.

'I think I'm depressed,' I tell Dr Stewart, who has known me forever. What I really mean is, I hope I am depressed. What I suspect is that I am having a breakdown of some kind. Physical and mental. I am terrified. Please let it be depression! There are pills for that.

'Why?'

I've had sex with a Polish man I don't even know the last name of. And have been thinking about nothing else since. I am nauseous and demented and exhausted. I feel, literally, insane.

'Oh, I just don't feel like myself lately.'

'In what way?'

In a sexual way.

'I can't think clearly. I feel preoccupied all the time. I don't sleep well. I don't have any appetite. I'm forgetful.'

'Those symptoms could be due to other causes. Is there any stress in your life?'

The proximity of a man who is not my husband. Who has made me a stranger to myself. Who has made all my certainties into nebulous nothings.

'Not really. Enjoy my job. Love my husband. Trying to have a baby.'

'How long have you been trying?'

Then he tells me I am just anxious about conceiving, and in any case, anti-depressants would not help the foetus, if a foetus came along. As if I care about a baby anymore!

'And my periods have been so odd, lately. Irregular and very light. Only spotting, really.'

'Oh? Perhaps you should have a pregnancy test then.'

On the way home, I feel dizzy, rearranging the future in my head. It was all so carefully laid out, and now it's as if I'm blind and someone has moved all the furniture in my house. Pregnant! Where is my joy? My hope? I tell myself to stop at Boots for a pregnancy test, but have forgotten to make that turning by the time the turning comes, and then it's too late. I'll buy one tomorrow, I tell myself.

I understand, at last, how the word unbalanced can be applied to a mental state. I feel vertigo in my core, and the earth's surface has liquefied. And none of these catastrophes matter to me. Because the most alarming truth is that I am actually vacant.

I start and stop all day. Pick up my shoes, then sit on the bed and stare out the window for a mysterious amount of time. Mysterious, because I have not timed my own spell of vagueness, and so have no idea really. Yesterday, while I was searching for some body lotion to put in my swim bag, I went into a dwam in front of the bathroom mirror, and when I resurfaced I was almost too late for swimming. When I was in the changing room, I stared at my breasts in the mirror. I think I have fallen in love with them. Quite arousing, to find proper breasts on one's chest after all these years. I see that I must be pregnant now. No need for a test, it's obvious. Just not like I thought it would be.

Maciek! There he sits, and here I swim, just like last Tuesday. Which feels like a year ago. He has no smile for me tonight – why? Just his serious black eyes. Like it never happened. What did happen? It seems so random. An accident. The shop, my nausea, the cold, the Gold Wasser. Hormones. My breasts led me astray. I can only account for that hour by thinking of it as a seizure. Like an epileptic fit. I was not, in my normal sense, present for the event. Though, of course, I have a clear memory of at least the beginning and end of it. I understand the word swoon now, and know one cannot be held responsible for anything that happens during a swoon. And I do not blame Maciek either. I was not a victim of him, but of my own body. I forgive myself, and will be extra vigilant from now on.

Did I kiss him? I believe I did not. Not properly.

I felt so weak, and he seemed so tall, so solid. I felt like a little girl, being led. His caravan is one of the older residential ones. Green and white, with a tiny door Maciek had to duck through.

Inside, it was dark and damp. No personal touches – no photos, or only one – of a young woman. No ornaments, no plants. There was a smell of mould and a sweet fruitiness. Instantly depressing. I loved it, it answered my own strange mood. He showed me the bottle of Gold Wasser. Like a dealer slyly revealing the cocaine, or a toddler proudly showing his finger painting. Both of these things. Illicit and innocent.

'Do you have a girlfriend?' I asked, though I knew the answer didn't matter at all.

He took off his trilby hat, and instantly looked exposed. I looked away for a second.

'No.'

'I'm married,' I said.

'Yes,' he said, after a moment.

He was silent then, and I was too. It was a good quiet, full of quietness. I remember wishing he didn't try to speak at all. It was all in his eyes, anyway. I held the bottle to the window. Same shape as a Jack Daniel's bottle. The label had a pink floral design on it and the words were in Polish. Inside the clear liquid, golden flakes shimmered. What kind of liquid suspends pieces of gold? Maciek had two small glasses and reached for the bottle, but I couldn't open my hands to give it to him just yet. It was dim, so he lit a candle.

'Better than using the electricity,' he said. 'And this house, this caravan, it is better in candlelight. Not so ugly.'

The candle smelled of some kind of berry, strawberry or raspberry, and I realised that is what I smelled when I entered. He must light candles often. The drink tasted, at first, of strong medicine mixed with Southern Comfort. Spicy and hot. A second after, my insides melted. It spread out, and even my sore breasts were relieved. I couldn't feel the flakes of gold going down. He made a toast in Polish, and I think I said cheers.

Then he took my empty glass away, and I let him undress me.

It was like he was undressing someone else, while I watched.

Ian is such a patient man, he will make a fine father. He is always considering my feelings. He's even letting my father help choose baby names, because I want him to. All Polish of course. Dear Dad. I have a photograph, small, black and white, of my father and some other Polish soldiers at the Major's Woods, near Invergordon. They look like they're on a break from working, perhaps on a farm. 1945 is scribbled on the back in pencil. Their shirtsleeves are rolled up, and they all look incredibly thin, with cigarettes dangling from their mouths. But they're laughing and clowning around. As if they're intoxicated, posing at a party. Perhaps the photographer was a young woman; they were flirting with her. Or perhaps every day, out of the war, was intoxicating. Even wives and families back home were not enough to entice some of these men home later, and they married locally, becoming bigamists.

Maciek has stopped looking at me. He's looking at the clock on the opposite wall. He'll never save one of us from drowning that way. He's sad today, he can't hide this, but this is a face made for sadness. The double-lidded eyes, so he always looks drowsy and reflective. The lean planes of his cheeks, no jolliness could ever thrive there. And his thin-lipped mouth, which I have seen smile only twice, both times in Tesco. He is, if such a thing is possible, physiologically suited for melancholy.

Like Dad. He seems to embrace sadness, wallow in it. He is sad without the usual shame men feel. I've read some Polish history, of course, and once I asked my father what would have been the solution, back in 1939.

'What would have saved Poland?'

'To have had different neighbours.'

Then his eyes filled with tears, even while he was smiling at me. Dad loves me. I've always felt this in a way that I don't feel from Mum. With Mum, I know I am loved for reasons; with Dad, I just feel loved. My aunt, Dad's sister, loves me too in that immediate physical way, even though she is the opposite of Dad every other way. She's chosen to be just Scottish, and hates it when Dad uses Polish words. She's never been back to Poland.

'Why would I want to go there?' she asks. 'It's nothing to me. I'm going to Tenerife, where at least the sun is shining and everyone speaks English and they sell fish and chips. You know where you are, in a place like Tenerife.'

The water feels different tonight; I feel more buoyant. My strokes are effortless. I feel at ease with myself. Why should that be such a rare occurrence? There's that music again. The same CD Maciek put on before, with the sad flute and the violin. I slow my rhythm automatically, to swim to it. I don't look at him. The chlorine stings my eyes and brings tears. I swim up and down, and no matter what I think about, I always come back to this: Everything is changing. I've betrayed my husband. I'm having a baby. I'm a pregnant adulterer. But somehow, at this moment of swimming, none of this affects me. I press my fingers together and curve my hands away from each other. Divide the water and pull myself body through it. My knees bend, my legs open so wide I feel a stretching ache. Then, in unison with my arms, I kick them straight and shoot ahead a little. There is so much pleasure in the efficiency of the body, don't you think?

In the changing room, I strip and dry myself. It only takes a minute. When Maciek suddenly enters my cubicle, it's so shocking I can't feel shocked. Didn't I latch the door? It's too quick for my heart to react, which is beating normally, ignoring the message from my eyes. I don't say anything; I can't. Maciek says nothing either. Just takes the towel from me and puts it down. The back wall of the cubicle is solid, part of the building, and Maciek pushes me against this. Not roughly. I feel detached still. Watching myself, and not even alarmed. Curious. Then the strangest thing happens. Without consulting myself, my arms pull his sad face down to mine and I am kissing him on the mouth. And my heart finally pounds so fast, I think I might be having a heart attack. What does kissing Maciek feel like? It feels like happiness, of course. What did you think?

Rose

Oh bloody hell, Sam's in love. Poor lamb. I totally recognise that look.

I've been fourteen too. His name was Andrew McKay, and I sat behind him in school. Couldn't take my eyes off the back of his head. God how I loved those short bristly blond hairs. Ached to touch that fuzzy bit of neck. His dad had a farm, and after the summer holidays, Andrew's skin was a kind of gold. Never did tell him how I felt. A new girl joined the class, one with proper boobs already, and she got Andrew, even though I warned her at lunch one day that he was mine. Which was wishful thinking, times a million.

I'm standing in my kitchen and blushing. What the hell happened to him? And why am I blushing? Maybe it's just another of those flushes. The hot flashbacks. The flush is still building. I sit down with my cup of tea and allow it to pass through me. This is what it feels like: a contraction, a wringing out, a wave. It has a rhythm and length, a beginning, middle and end. And when it's over, I feel like my youth has receded that much further, left me higher and drier. Like an old mini-dress I can't even remember wearing.

When I'm talking to friends, I always say I don't care about menopause. I say not caring is the saving grace of middle age. My younger self may be beached now, but I say: So long, sucker! Who gives a fuck?

Well, I do. Duh.

The real surprise, the real saving grace of middle age, is sex. As if, in its death throes, as my eggs diminish to zero, my libido's throwing all caution to the wind. It's hollering at the top of its pornographic voice: Give me sex! Many men, men I don't even know but please god, not my husband!!! Fat willies! Tongues!!! God, even a hand to hold. A kiss. One second of one kiss.

A first kiss, oh sweet jesus please, one more first kiss before I croak.

I drink my cooling tea and it feels like a molten core is being cooled.

Harry's already gone to work, and there's Sam now, slamming the door on his way out, without a goodbye, never mind a kiss. Poor lovelorn sod, he's forgotten his dinner money.

I check my emails one last time, and find Alpin in my inbox, like an unexploded bomb. I'm late. Work starts in ten minutes, and I haven't even brushed my teeth yet. Our last emails have been numerous, fevered, and worse – *I love you, I love you, I love you,* ***I miss you***.

There's a seriousness that was absent during our literal affair. Virtual love is tons more intense, I'm telling you. I click to open his email.

Darling. She knows.

Shit!

Shit shit shit! Didn't he delete our emails? Moron! No time to think about it. Anyway, she's in Leith. Not like I'm going to bump into her walking down the road. I race out of the house, teeth still furry. On the way down Chapel Street, I'm surprised by the Christmas decorations strung across the road. Very un-magic in the daylight.

Shit! Christmas!

More than anything else, even more than my obsession with Alpin, my ability to forget Christmas, to be *annoyed* by Christmas, is the strongest proof of what's happening to me hormonally. I am becoming a man! Men hate Christmas too. I used to make

Christmas cakes in September, for Christ sake, and this year it's store bought, and I haven't even bothered with cards. What'll become of me? I've no fucking idea. None. I don't give a damn about my house. My husband – a good man – I despise. My oldest friends, the ones I still hear from, just irritate me. The thought of Christmas makes me want to kill myself. I just don't have room anymore, to care about things like three for twos at Boots. No time! Let someone else – the next wife, the next mother – deal with those things.

It's strange, because I do feel like myself, despite all this. Perhaps, as the oestrogen ebbs, my former self is uncurling from whatever dark corner it's been hiding in, these past three decades. It fits my new looser skin perfectly, my true self, my rightful life. It's why I feel like shrugging off all these other things. Irrelevant, silly house and husband! Ridiculous and false Christmas spirit!

She knows!

As I enter Kiltearn Primary, I can smell the excitement of children in their last week before Christmas. It's not sweet, and their giggles and screeches aren't sweet either – their excitement makes them tired and strained, and they all talk too fast, laugh too loud. Forget their manners and say mean things to each other. And their teachers are strained too. Even us dinner ladies. Listen to us. We all sound nervous, actually.

She knows!

Then from the hall, come the voices of the younger ones, rehearsing for the nativity, and 'Silent Night' creeps out of the room, down the halls, under the doors of classrooms, into the kitchen and stops, for a minute, everything. Listen. Under their high angelic voices, you can hear the whole school exhale.

I remember now about Christmas. This is what it is for me, has always been:

Children singing 'Silent Night'.

Where have I put the box with Sam's stocking? I wonder if he has hair yet. Pubes, armpit hair. Can't remember last time I saw him naked. I'm going to buy him the Xbox he keeps on about.

He'll be well surprised and pleased. We've already told him he's not getting it. And I'll buy a bottle of malt for Harry.

Christmas used to be fun.

She knows!

Maciek

Christmas Eve in Krakow. Cracow. Hello Cracow! Maciek is back. It's been eight months, you have missed me? I don't miss you much. Yes, yes, it is good to hear voices like mine, but for an hour, I feel very strange. Travel home does this thing to me, always. Reminds me there are so many worlds. Everyone always busy and rushing, thinking their world is the only world, the important world, but this is not so. I feel dizzy, sick in my stomach. And here, there is so much of my past. I am not happy, to be home. I am still too much in Scotland.

Then, because I need to relax a little, I drink vodka in a café. Beautiful Polish vodka. Scotland, it fades a bit. Every swallow of vodka, less Evanton, less caravan. Even Ania, she begins to go. I can see Rynek Glowny Square from my seat. Look at it: None of the buildings match, except they all need paint. Like old people who are very poor; quiet old people, wearing different clothes but all grey and all in tatters. And some need to be held up by others, they are so old. But dignified, too. Krakow is never saying: Sorry, sorry about the way I look. Krakow says: Here I am. I am not ashamed I have seen some bad times. Look at my flower sellers, if the grey is too sad.

I count twenty-three flower stalls before I give up. I buy some roses and catch the train home to my Ciotka Agata.

At first, everyone wants to talk to me, to hug and kiss me.

'Maciek! Maciek, old man.'

'When are you coming back?'

'What the fuck does Scotland have that Poland does not?'

'We miss you, you bastard!'

'Got a woman there, eh? Getting any?'

'Give me your bag,' commands Ciotka Agata like she is in bad mood, and yes, she has tears.

My bag is heavy with presents I bring from Scotland. Tartan pottery mugs and plates, books with fold-out castles, half-bottles of Glenmorangie. I pass these around, and everybody opens these and talks at once. You would not look at me now and think: Poor Maciek. No brothers or sisters or parents, lives alone in damp caravan with smell of gas and furry stains on bathroom wall. No. I have a big family. A loud talking, big hugging, wet kissing, always arguing, crying out loud family. Did I say a lot of laughing too? Laughing, laughing till tears.

This is the house I come to after my mother, she dies. Nothing much is different now. Ciotka Agata does not believe in always change, change, change. Same red velvet wallpaper in living room, same photograph of Jozef Pilsudski w Zakopanem above the same sofa.

Because it's Christmas Eve, we eat fresh carp, the king of all the fish in all the lakes. Ciotka Agata, she keeps these carp in her bathtub until today. Best way to keep them. I miss her food. She is a very good cook, Agata. Nobody cooks the same.

In this family, except for me, we marry young. There are seven children here, and three babies. A few teenagers too. It is hard to remember all the names, and I keep thinking: Maciek, you must bring more presents next time. Everyone is talking, talking, talking, at same time as eat, and the babies cry a little. They are passed round the table, so even I hold a baby. Boy, girl, I don't know. The baby looks at me and cries. I try to make a funny face and the baby screams, so I pass it to another cousin. It is very warm in the kitchen, where we eat. Warm and smelling of people and food. I take a photograph of us, but I can't get everyone in. Only pieces. I start to feel full, not just of food, but everything. One cousin, he drinks too much, starts to sing, but it is a teasing song. A mean song about something silly that happens a long time ago. Another cousin, the one he teases, she throws her wine at him, and Ciotka Agata stands up and pretends to scold but there is a giggle in her eyes. Everyone, laughing. So much laughter and red faces and if the babies are still crying, nobody notices.

I start to want to be alone, so I can remember this, understand this. It is not always easy for me, to enjoy what is happening. I am too slow, perhaps.

I sleep at last in the room where all my boxes are, the ones with all my things from my flat inside them. My books, CDs, some coats and shoes. Some pots and pans, dishes and cups. A box of photographs, and little things like gifts from Agata. A scarf that Marja give to me one birthday. I am thirty-seven and my life is only what fits inside these boxes. What are things? But they disturb me. I sleep facing window, away from boxes.

The next day, I see Marja. Marja, who I leave Poland to avoid.

I'm on the tram, and there she is, on the street. She walks with her old walk, like she doesn't need to be anywhere for one day or ten, and I tell the tram man to stop. I run through some old snow. My shoes are not snow shoes and every step, my feet get wetter.

'Marja!'

She stops and waits for me, with her old smile. And her old laugh. As if nothing has changed. One time we have sex at a party, on a pile of coats. I am very drunk, and fall off the coat mountain, and she laughs this same way. And we sing that night, all the long walk home, down Grodzka Street. So now I give her a hug, despite everything. A big hug and a kiss, here on the street. How can I help myself? She is so *ladny*, Marja. So warm.

'Maciek! It's been a long time.'

'How are you, Marja?'

'I am fine, Maciek.'

'You have a new boyfriend? I hear you are with Tomas now.'

'No! Tomas got the shove last month.' Marja giggles as if Tomas leaving is a joke, and I laugh too, even though I don't get the joke. 'I have a new man. Nicholas. A Greek man, from the university. Studies Latin. Very handsome.'

'Oh! That's nice,' I say.

'I'm bad, aren't I?'

'No, no. You are you.'

'Are you still mad at me? Don't be angry, Maciek.'

'I'm not,' I say. 'I'm confused.'

She kisses me, puts her tongue in my mouth, just like that.

'Thanks, darling Maciek. You were always a darling. I think you are still my favourite. I just can't be serious, it's terrible. Maybe one day.'

'Yes? Maybe when you are eighty-five.'

'Will you marry me then? When I am an old woman, so fat no other man will have me?'

'Yes. Of course, Marja.' I smile, and it hurts that she believes this smile.

So we go to her flat, which is only one street away, and the Greek will not be back for three hours. We take all our clothes off. In three seconds, we are naked. No small talk with Marja. No: Do you want to, I don't know, do you? The room smells, but I don't want to think of what. Another man's cigarette smoke, his after shave. I stop thinking.

After, she wants to make me a meal. I can stay two more hours, she says. But I don't want to eat. I don't want to stay. I put my clothes back on. She wraps herself in a blanket and sits up, watching me.

'So, Maciek, you haven't told me. Are you in love with anyone now?'

'In love?'

'You are! Look at you! You are blushing.'

'Don't laugh.'

'Sorry. It is good you are in love. It is what you are good at. And she is in love with you?'

'I don't know. Maybe. A little.'

Then Marja gets out of bed, walks up to me naked, and buttons up my coat. Like I am four years old. She kisses me goodbye at the door. A loud lips closed smack.

'Take care of her, Maciek. And take care of yourself!'

Three days after Christmas, I walk through the Cloth Hall, buy some presents. An amber necklace for Ania. A knife with an amber handle for Sam. Ciotka Agata, she gives me a box full of food to bring to Scotland. I tell her about the shelves in Tesco, with all the Polish food, but she doesn't believe me. She has her worried look for me, and my youngest cousin, he is angry that I am leaving again so soon. But I am glad it is over. It is eating too much rich cake, an especially wonderful cake. It makes you want to sleep. I want to see Ania. The last time was in the little room for changing, at the swimming pool. We do not talk then. Her kiss. Her kiss.

On the plane at night, I look out of the window at the lights below. Lights that crowd up to each other. Seen from a plane, it is very obvious. People, they want to be near other people.

I take the bus from Edinburgh airport to Haymarket, then a train to Inverness, and a bus to Evanton. I do not speak to anyone. English sounds strange, the first day back. I keep my eyes closed but never quite fall asleep. I worry about leaving Ciotka Agata's box somewhere. The shelf above my seat, the floor by my feet.

Walking up my path, I see Mr McKenzie, the landlord.

'Hello,' I say. 'Please, I hope you have a good Christmas. Yes?'

'Aye. A quiet one.'

'Good. Mr McKenzie?'

'Aye?'

'Sorry, if you are busy, but I want to remind you. There is still a smell of gas in my caravan. Even outside the caravan now.'

'No. You're wrong, there's nothing wrong with the gas.'

I am so tired. I shut my eyes for a second.

'Come and smell this gas, please. You will see.' I do not speak to him like this before.

'There is nothing wrong with the gas.' He says this very slowly, like I am stupid, and then he turns to go into his house. At his door, he turns, looks right at me and says: 'And that hat looks daft. You look like a dafty.'

'Bitch! I tell you, there is a gas smell!'

He walks into his house and shuts his door so fast, the silver Christmas wreath falls onto his steps.

'*Kurwa!*' I shout to his door. '*Kurwa mac!*'

I look around for something to break, or throw. Then suddenly, the anger is gone, and I am just tired and hungry again.

I go to the shop to buy milk and bread and a bottle of vodka. I hate Scottish bread, the vodka is not great, but the milk it is beautiful. I also like the bacon here. After a while, my caravan is fine. I light candles, I light the stove to heat a tin of soup, and I listen to the radio. Still mostly Christmas songs. I think to myself: Maciek! Why are you here? Why?

I hope that she will come, and then she does. It is as if I make it happen.

'Maciek,' she says, after opening my door.

'Please, Ania. It is good to see you, come in,' I say, and I feel shy. This caravan, I want it to be a nicer place for her.

'How was Krakow?'

'It is good. Very good to see my family.'

'And they are all well?'

'Yes.' I think of Marja's mirrors for a minute, and my mouth tastes sour.

'Maciek, I have some news.'

'Sit down Ania. I can make you some tea. It is good news?'

'Good news, Maciek.' But in her eyes is sad news. And it feels familiar, like I am always waiting for this sad news.

If she asks for tea, I make her a special cup of tea, with the raspberry my Ciotka gave me. But she wants juice. I pour two glasses. Give her a glass, and I sit down too. Not next to her, but my caravan is so small our knees they almost touch. I keep my knees from touching hers because something, I can see, is wrong.

'Alright, Ania. Tell me your good news please.'

'Ok.' She sighs, and her face is pink. 'I will just say it quick, and then it will be over. I'm pregnant.'

I make a noise, but not a word.

'With my husband's baby. I'm four months pregnant.'

Still, no words from me, but for different reason. I feel cold. And tired. I feel like I'm asleep and this is a very bad dream.

'I didn't know I was pregnant. Not till just before Christmas.'

'Oh,' I say. 'I understand,' I say. An ache begins above my right eye, a sharp painful ache.

'I'm sorry, Maciek.'

'I have a Christmas gift for you, from home.'

'Oh Maciek, that's so kind of you! I don't have anything for you.'

'You don't need to give me anything.' It's hard to speak, but I do. I get the gift from my bag. I don't know what else to do. To say.

'Open it later.'

'Thank you.'

'You are happy to have this baby? You love your husband?'

'I want the baby. I won't leave my husband.' She holds my hand. Holds one hand, in both of her hands.

I lift my glass to drink, but my throat says no. No swallowing just now.

'Ok Ania. Please, I understand. It is over. Yes?'

'Aye. I'm so sorry. I won't come here again.'

I can't look at her. I order myself: Don't cry Maciek!

'Fine. Goodbye then.'

'Maciek, I am so . . .'

Then, it is like with Mr McKenzie, and I can only think: *Kurwa!* Fuck this!

'Oh, just fuck off, Ania. Just. Go.'

'Maciek, I came to say I'm sorry. But please let's not part this way.'

Kurwa! Now she is crying!

'Just fuck off!' is all I say again. I sound like a teenager, sulking. I hate myself, but I hate her more.

She puts her not empty juice glass on the table, and stands. Puts my gift in her pocket. Walks to the door. Her coat is still on.

'Don't go. Ania. I love you! I love you! I *love* you!'

This is terrible. I hate myself more. She does not turn, so I go to her and hug her tight, from behind.

She finally turns around, and I let go of her. I am not a teenager. I am angry, yes, but I remember to be an adult now. I take her hand and I think to shake it, but then I bend over it, like this, and I am kissing it.

'If we must say goodbye, then we say goodbye like this. I hope you have a nice baby, Ania. And a good life.'

'Thank you. Goodbye Maciek,' she says, very seriously. Her face wet.

Then I start to open the door for her.

I still hold her very small and cold hand. Her other hand, she has on her stomach.

And then we take our clothes off and we fuck like there is no tomorrow.

In a million years, not one tomorrow.

HOGMANAY

Maciek

The last day of the year. A night of drink, drink, drink. And parties. Frost already, only 9:30. Maybe black ice later, and cars in ditches. Sirens and fireworks. I am going to a party in the house of some Polish people I meet at work. The couple who clean at Dingwall Leisure Centre. I can walk, it is only ten minutes away. I like them, a sweet couple. They hold hands when they leave work, to catch the bus. They talk in Polish together at work, but quietly.

I will take them a bottle of vodka from home, and also this piece of torte Ciotka Agata made for me.

But then here she is.

Ania, very cold and pink. I think she runs here. She reaches inside my heart and crawls in, and this is easy because when I see her, my chest opens up. No words.

No words, and this sweet couple will understand if I am late.

Sam

Pissed as fuck. Dad gie me some beer, then I drank the Grouse bottla half in my room. Stole it yonks ago. Like they'd notice anything.

Listening to The Dykeenies.

Quite nice, being rat arsed.

I'm heading to Maciek's. Gie him his Christmas prezzie. He's gonna love it. Bet he's just sitting in on his own, poor bastard.

Maciek's sound. I'll get the craic with him. He'll maybe give me a dram.

But at his caravan, in his window: her face.

Crap! But beast that he's getting some.

Ania

'I'm just going to pop down to Mum and Dad's, see if they're ok. Won't be long.'

'Back before the bells?'

'Aye, back before then,' I assure my good husband, put on my wool coat, walk out of my house, and run to the caravan park. Some kids are already lighting fireworks behind the bus shelter, and one of them shouts after me: 'Where's the fire?'

My breasts really hurt, running like this. I'm holding them as I run. I don't care who sees me.

Later, I explain about conjugating verbs, because Maciek hardly ever does and should learn. The conjugations of run. And love: Love, loved, loving. To love, will love. Then, because I am half-dressed, and he is naked, and the caravan is lit by a dozen candles, I think about the word itself. Conjugate. Conjugal.

Rose

'Where're you going?' But it's too late, and the door slams in a Sam way. Stupidly hard. In his new stupid tough way.

I'm a bit worried, but Harry just shrugs and opens some fizzy wine.

Not champagne, but that's fine by me. The good stuff would be wasted on me. On the pair of us. We're not like that, me and Harry.

Tonight, it feels wrong to be here. We should be bringing in the New Year in Leith. Mum's crowded kitchen. Harry's rowdy friends. Sam would be with us, not running off like that. Like he hates us.

Nothing's right but Harry. And even he's pretty bloody strange.

I emailed Alpin earlier.

I'm scared.

Ditto, baby.

JANUARY

Evanton

Christmas puddings marked down to half price in the co-op. Christmas cracker toys in the slushy gutter. Gossip of alcohol-fuelled moments circulates the morning kitchens of housewives. Children sledging on what remains of the snow in the schoolyard. The Christmas tree by the car park is now so lopsided, the star on top can be reached by eleven-year-olds. People have a tired, yet quietly triumphant, look to their faces. Battle weary warriors, returning undefeated from yet another Christmas.

And of course, everyone's skin is thinner – Christmas has sapped their usual barriers, and the secrets are closer to the surface. The woman just leaving the co-op, for instance. She greets her neighbour and they talk of the January sales, as if she has not just had the diagnosis. She cannot look at the reduced puddings without thinking: I'll not be here when this season comes again. She talks like she cares about sales, but her friend notices this other truth without knowing the actual facts, and touches her arm.

And the fourteen-year-old girl in the bus shelter, laughing loudly with her friends, had sex with four boys over the Christmas holidays. This is not a secret, as the boys have re-told their luck. But her depression is a secret. The way she feels about her own body is a secret. But not so secret her mother hasn't noticed that she's left off the make-up this last week.

Everyone has secrets. It is just harder in January to conceal them, and if people feel a little unreal this time of year, or that their friends seem a little off, it is only the strain of concealment. Rose gets headaches, planning her escape. Ania forgets the right times to smile at her husband.

Sam

I walk into the living room and there's Mum, at the computer again, and she immediately hits the delete button. What's she like? Probably thinks deleted emails really vanish. Has she really never visited the deleted folder? I know all about her and Alpin. Pathetic, is all I can say. Middle-aged twats. I do MSN and Bebo, so after Mum leaves the room, I log on and read what people have been saying to Jake, my alter ego on Bebo. Quite a lot, actually, and so they should. Jake's well good. Then I notice Roksana's name and click on it, and there she is, messaging him. Shit! No fucking way!

I've always pictured her in a house with no computer, and lots of strange food. I've seen her parents; her dad has a moustache and her mum wears a shell suit for fuck sake. I don't hold this against her, like. I mean, look at my parents.

But this is proper bad. Roksana *likes* Jake. The Jake I created one rainy boring afternoon last summer. Jake is the oldest of seven kids. They've no parents, and been adopted by a rich stockbroker he can't name for security reasons. He's fifteen, shags around, plays drums, swears, drinks and is tall. Everything he says is either sarcastic or funny. Jake is a basically a dick. Roksana should be reading something wholesome by the fire, while fingering the dolphin earrings I gave her for Christmas.

Then Mum comes back and starts in. What is it with her always wanting us to talk? I watch her mouth move, and ignore her; pretend I can't hear her. Easy with the iPod on. Hope she'll go away.

'Sam. Sam! Please take off your headphones, I am trying to talk to you.'

'What.'

'Are you hungry? I'm starving. Fancy a bacon buttie?'

'No thanks Mum.'

'You sure?'

'Sure.'

'But you didn't have breakfast, did you?'

'So what?'

She looks out the window for a minute, sighs this sigh, then:

'I'm freezing. Are you warm enough? Will I light the fire?'

'Whatever.'

'What does that mean? Are you cold or not?'

'Not.'

'It's stopped raining. Why don't you run outside and play awhile?'

Why don't I run outside and play? Does she think I'm seven?

She does my head in. To get her off my case, I put on my jacket and head down the street. I spot Maciek, looking ill. Or hungover. Totally know what that feels like since Hogmanay. Like you need to puke but you can't move. For about ten days.

Maciek's already inside his caravan by the time I get there, but when I knock, nothing. I call his name – but still, no answer. I can see someone moving behind the curtains. I knock again.

'Hey, Maciek! You in there? It's me.'

What the fuck.

Then the door opens, and he says: 'Sam. Sorry. Come in.'

The place looks wrecked. *He* looks wrecked.

'Growing a beard, Maciek?'

'Oh!' He feels his chin, like he's only just noticed the bristles. God, what I'd do for some facial hair.

'You think I look the handsome man with a beard? Maybe I stop shaving, grow this beard.'

'Are you mental? No. Beards look tinky. Hippy-ish.'

'Ok. Ok.' He looks a bit sad.

I put the kettle on, since he's not bothering. He's yawning, and scratching his belly. It's pretty gross, actually. And the place reeks.

'So, Maciek, what's up?'

'What is up? I am cooked, that is what.'

'Cooked? Is that Polish for hungover?'

'It is English for cooked. I am in love, and she is married.'

'Well, I told you, that day. She's like, married to my English teacher.'

'Yes, I remember.' He rubs his eyes, and I make us both cups of tea. 'And she is having a baby.'

'Crap. Yours?'

'No. Her husband's.'

'Bugger. Mind if I make a bacon sandwich, Maciek? Only I'm starving.'

'Please!'

'Want one?'

'No.'

'So, what's it mean now? Her having this baby?'

'I don't know. Maybe no difference.'

I turn on the gas hob, light it, pour oil in the pan, flop the bacon in. Right away, the place smells better. And I am, actually, starving.

'So what's the problem? She's pregnant and married, but you don't need to marry her and have babies, do you? Can you not just shag her now and then? You'd probably go off her after a while, anyway. If yous two were married, like.'

'You think? We can be happy – just being lovers some times?'

His face, right now, is exactly like this dog I used to have. No pride. Totally begging for a bone, anything. Like me hoping for Roksana to give me . . . anything. A look. No one ever tells you how much love sucks.

'Actually, I haven't a clue. Sorry mate. Just thought you might give it a try. Nothing to lose, yeah?'

I like the bacon nice and crispy. The sandwich is perfect, but Maciek is crap company today. And the Roksana thing is kind of still bothering me. I notice that Maciek is wearing the shirt I gave him for Christmas, but it's not enough. I still feel boab. It's like there's two camps: People like me and Maciek, wanting something. And the people who don't give a fuck.

Ania

I need him. All I can think about is him. But equally – I don't want to get caught. I need Ian too. I can't tell how careless I'm being, because I've lost all sense of normality. Every minute of every day, a tightrope. And I am so dizzy, so very dizzy. I've never laughed so much in my life, but by god I am tired. Every time I sit, I fight sleep. People talking, or myself driving, watching a movie – I just don't care. Quite exhilarating, not caring. I don't know anything anymore. Which makes life, suddenly, very simple. If dangerous.

This has been my first hellish Christmas. Of course, I already knew it was hell on struggling marriages – January 17th is officially the most popular day of the year for filing for divorce – but somehow I never took in what this meant. The grinding ache of relentless cheer. The grating of other people's happiness.

My baby has begun. It's over four months. It has eyes, ears, fingernails. No one can tell, by looking. Ian likes to touch my belly and talk to it already, which embarrasses me. I don't know why. It's quite sweet, really.

Tonight at Rose and Harry's session, things progress at an alarming rate. Well, it alarms them, but it's old hat to me. Couples frequently hurtle forward and imagine that by changing their circumstances, their inner turmoil will magically disperse. Sorted, they think, and cross things off a list.

Things To Do To Avoid Divorce

1. Foreign holiday with no kids.
2. Special gifts.
3. Dinners in nice restaurants.
4. Move to new place for fresh start.
5. See Relate counsellor.
6. A temporary separation.

'I think what we need is a brief time apart, just to get some perspective,' says Rose. 'After all this time together, we seem to be locked into a negative pattern.'

'You really want me to move out?' Harry whispers, his eyes looking pink already.

'Actually, I was thinking I'd move out for a while Harry. Don't you think it's best that way? Sam needs stability and his dad, and I'd be nearby for him.'

That familiar pause.

'Are you in touch with Alpin?'

'No! I just want some space.'

The queen of euphemisms! I don't say this, of course. Lately it's occurred to me that Rose actually hates me. She probably hates anyone understanding her.

'Space to meet up with him?'

'No, Harry. Really. Stop being paranoid. There's no one else! But this way you'd be free to meet someone who might love you . . . properly. Anyway, we've already said all this. Why are you acting like this? We decided to split up a month ago.'

They did?

'Aye, aye. I didn't think we really meant it. Thought you'd forgotten about that.'

I suddenly feel almost invisible. Definitely redundant. I guess it means I've done my job, if they can communicate without me.

Rose laughs giddily then, and Harry laughs suddenly too, like they often do, these daring couples that imagine freedom. The imagined prospects! Another chance to get it right! Who wouldn't be almost delirious?

Must be careful. Did I leave my phone on the table? Did I leave it on silent, so Ian won't pick it up to answer? Did I remind Maciek to not ring tonight?

'We can be friends, Harry. We can be anything we want. There're no rule books, and a million different kinds of possible relationships. We can be better friends than we ever were husband and wife.'

They agree on a six-month separation, and will visit me once a month during this. Apparently my usefulness is not over. They need my presence in order to say certain things.

I'm glad when they leave. I am tired and yes, I am confused. All the advice I would normally have given to Rose and Harry suddenly seems glib. Besides, I find it hard to concentrate on them. I have lost confidence. I've lost interest in other people. That is what Maciek has done to me. If this is love, I want a refund. Where's my notebook? I start a new list.

Bad Things That Can Happen To Lovers

1. Loss of reasoning ability (effective immediately).
2. Loss of personality. One ceases to recognise oneself.
3. Loss of confidence.
4. Loss of integrity.
5. Loss of sleep.
6. Loss of appetite.
7. Subsequent loss of looks and health.
8. Loss of reputation and respectability. (Can lead to end of career and social life.)
9. Disease and/or pregnancy.
10. Loss of moral fibre (related to number 2).
11. Loss of sense of humour. (When it relates to the love object.)

I suppose, in a way, loving Maciek could be seen as a professional development course, designed to enhance my counselling skills. Maybe I'd qualify for a grant from Relate, to pay for all expenses incurred by having an affair. Including protecting me from possible loss of income, should my husband leave me.

Later, back in my spotless and quiet house, I am not thinking about him, because there is no point at all in thinking about someone who cannot be a part of your perfect life. And my life is potentially perfect. On paper, it looks very good indeed. No weak seams, no thinning walls.

Go away, I tell him in my mind. *Go away!*

In the next instant, I'm checking my phone for a message from him. It's been more than two days since I last heard from him, and I'm feeling a bit panicky. It's like love is a substance with volume, taking up space, but seeping out with every heartbeat away from the lover. The love tank needs to be re-filled often. What would happen if it just ran out? How do people get out of bed and go to work, on empty?

I go to bed with the father of my baby. He's reading *Psychologies*, a self-help magazine. Don't ask me why, he's not like that really. Is he?

'How's the baby?' he asks, putting his magazine down.

'Fine,' I say. 'How was your day?'

He tells me about the schoolwork he has to do, and the staff gossip, about the discovery of the maths teacher and learning support lady in the storeroom. About the boy in fourth year he spotted today on the high street, who is probably psychotic and always spits, and the first-year girl who is probably anorexic. And the extra forms he now has to fill in. The endless stress.

I make many attentive sympathetic noises.

'Oh dear!'

'That's awful!'

'What little monsters!'

I used to like these windows into his world, though I would hate to be a teacher.

Finally he pauses and asks: 'How was your day?'

'Well, this morning I went for a lovely walk up Fyrish – did you know there's still snow up there? And at the top, I was alone and there was a roe deer just over the other side of the monument. He stood completely still for ages, and we just stared at each other. Then at counselling tonight, I lost a couple.'

'Oh dear. Ah Ania.'

'Aye, I tried, but . . .' Weirdly, saying it out loud is almost making me cry. I wasn't even thinking about it before. But I hate it when a couple does that. Gives up.

'So sad! Are you upset sweetie?'

'A bit, I guess.'

'You shouldn't take it personally. You did your best. They were probably miserable together.'

'Still.'

'Come here, you.'

Ian has stopped wanting sex, but he's found a gentle way to hold my new shape close, to hold us both. He is a good man and I love him.

The next morning, before I am awake enough to remember that I must not think of Maciek, I text him:

Come 2 me 4 brkfst.

This is the first time I've initiated something, and such a dangerous thing! I have the ingredients for a fry up out, but we never even make it to the kitchen. I think what I love best of all, is the way he takes me as if he can't help himself, as if I've put a spell on him. There is nothing gentle or considerate in his embrace; at first, he is not thinking of me at all. He is not thinking. I'm still in my nightie and robe, both of which he hoists up.

When Ian's car pulls up, we are both off the sofa instantly. My nightie is where it should be again, and my robe belted. Maciek's jeans are zipped, and his shirt buttoned. Hat on.

Maciek gives me a look I can't at first fathom. Calm? But how can he be calm? We are about to be killed.

I am terrified, and my voice is bright and hard.

'Ian! Did you forget something?'

'The reflective essays from the fifth years. Oh! Hello!' as he spots Maciek, who is pulling on his coat. I am about to throw up.

'Good morning,' Maciek says to Ian, then turns to me.

'So, I'll phone you,' he says, looking straight at me with that fathomless look, 'when the pipes I order, they are here.'

I just stare at him.

'Pipes?' asks Ian, mouth frozen in an odd half smile.

'The pipes to fix central heating,' explains Maciek. Then he yawns, actually yawns the yawn of the utterly innocent. My heart swells. I'm going to burst open.

'Thanks. Oh, this is Maciek, Ian. Mum gave me his number, for that dodgy radiator in the spare room. I told you, didn't I?'

Maciek leaves, and I walk into the kitchen and offer my husband a late breakfast. The lot – eggs, toast, bacon, black pudding.

I met Ian when I was in primary one, at Kiltearn. He was smaller than me, and peed himself the first day. I can't look at him and see him, any more than I can look at Evanton and really see it. Evanton is just Evanton, and I don't know if Ian is handsome or ugly. I suspect he is in between.

'More bacon?' I ask, because I know this about him – he likes bacon.

Rose

Harry knows me. He doesn't actually *notice* me, but he knows me better than anyone. I'm always myself with him. And he's right – I always do get what I want. I wanted Alpin, and now I've fucking got him. She's kicked him out. I've told Harry I'm moving out to my own place. Now what?

Try to act normal, seems good advice. Brush teeth, say good morning, make breakfast, smile, breathe. But everything I do these days is done self-consciously. This might be the last time I hoover this floor, water this plant, wash these grey y-fronts, sleep next to my husband. Kiss him. Call to him:

'Dinner's ready!'

Shout up the stairs to Sam:

'Turn that bloody music down!'

You always know when the first time is, but how can you know when it's the last time? My voice, to my own ears, sounds false and loud. And I hardly sleep at all. I've forgotten how sleep goes.

Everything is in slow motion. I take the Christmas tree down, even though I know I should wait one more day for good luck. I just can't bear it a minute longer. If I pause, nothing will happen for the rest of my life. And the sound of time rushing is a roar in my head. I lug the tree through the house, shedding needles everywhere. No one offers to help me, as usual. Dump it out by the bin.

Harry's watching a football game and Sam's in his room doing god knows what. Despite the way I feel, there's this funny hum of normality. It's as if I've not told them. Like I dreamt saying those words. Maybe they're giving me a second chance. If I don't leave, they'll pretend I never said I would.

No.

I write a to-do list as if it's a to-save-my-life list. I make a dozen phone calls, and by noon I have paid the first month's rent on a tiny furnished cottage on the Back Road. I've some savings, it'll last a few months. After that, who knows. I allow myself a sandwich and cup of coffee, then grab my list and drive to Inverness, to the big Tesco. Everything God created is in this Tesco. I buy bath towels, tea towels, sheets, a duvet, a tea pot, a cafetiere, a vase, flowers, candles, plates, bowls, cups, cutlery, shampoo, soap, washing powder, washing-up liquid, butter, olive oil, oranges, sardines (for my bones), oatmeal, yoghurt, milk, salad, tomatoes, three kinds of cheeses, six bottles of red wine, orange juice, bananas, honey, eggs, oatcakes (not bloating bread). All this comes to £176.23. A whole new life begun for so little! I put these in my boot, and walk into Currys. Buy a small television and DVD player, small CD player, small hoover and a kettle (not the posh kind). £212.76. Still a bargain.

It's only 2:30. I drive to my new cottage, which is painted white inside, and which looks over fields of winter stubble. I unload my new possessions. By 4:30 I've put my shopping away, put the flowers in a vase, rearranged the furniture, contemplated my new nest, shivered with excitement and genuine cold, made another list of things still to get and do (table lamps, throws, post office address change form, electric radiator, order coal) and by 5:10, I'm home again. Before I go inside, I text Alpin. His wife filed for divorce today. He'll be in bits.

Nw base camp estblishd.

Drlng! U r genius.

Hurry!

Xx

Xxx

Xxxx

And so on. But I lost that easy happy feeling with Alpin a while ago. I wonder if he's as nervous and tired as I am. I try to get back that buzzy way he used to make me feel – but nope. All gone, for now anyway. Hopefully the actual sight of him will re-ignite it. A proper full-on snog should do the job. The plan is that he'll just be staying with me while he looks for his own place, a flat where his kids can visit him. At least he doesn't need to worry about work. He works from home editing something or other online. To tell the truth, I'm not exactly sure what he does. Or whether he snores. Or what he likes for breakfast.

Harry's still in the living room, television blaring; Sam's still upstairs, music blaring. But there's an air of subdued panic now. And neglect. The fire's not been lit, and the house is chilly. The lunch dishes still sit on the kitchen table, and actually, so do the breakfast dishes. There's some rice crispies spilled on the floor, and the milk has been left out. I know these are all material objects, but still – they're all looking at me reproachfully.

'I'm home, boys!'

I think they grunt in reply, but over the television and music it's hard to tell. And why are they in separate rooms? If they're worried, why aren't they at least in the same room? Shit! Intensely annoying, the way they still manage to make me feel protective. But they'll be fine here, without me. Better than fine. They'll learn to be less lazy, more self-sufficient. They'll become closer. They will!

I begin to clear up, put the dirty dishes in the dishwasher, but it's still clean from the night before, and suddenly I'm just about falling over, I'm so tired. It seems surreal, my new cottage. As for Alpin, I think I must have made him up.

Sam comes down the stairs, with the same look he used to have after naps. Dazed and all cuddly looking. Gives me a blank look, glances into the living room, and turns back to me.

'Where's the tree?'

Before I can answer, Harry pops his own dazed face round the door, and asks:

'Hey, why'd you take the tree down?'

I know the answer, I have the words – there are so many – but hell! I can't say any of them.

Outside, the wind is suddenly shrill, and I can hear sleet hit the kitchen window. Good. I hope it blizzards. I ring Lily, I'm that desperate, and she's there like a shot, equally desperate, with two bottles of red. But by midnight, I am praying for her to go home.

FEBRUARY

Evanton

The days are longer, everyone comments on this, but February is the real heart of winter. Uncannily, it is also the heart of summer. A muggy still morning broken by a hail storm. A month of extremes, and people are moody. The moodiest are the village guardians. The ones who stay at home, and the ones who were born here; the rocks around which everyone else swirls. These quiet, strong individuals often pick fights in February. It just gets to be too much. Too many days indoors, with other people, trying to get along. It is such a relief, the sound of breaking glass, slamming doors. The satisfaction of finally saying it out loud – fuck off. Piss off.

Of course, this leads to other fights, till half the village is not speaking to the other half. Sensitive souls get their feelings hurt more easily, but even callous people cry in February, surprised by the sudden slap of hurt. Harry responds to hurt with defensive indifference, and Sam too. Their family splits soundlessly. People who wonder why there are so many wars have not paid enough attention to families in February. If families cannot survive harmoniously, what chance do countries have? The real wonder is that there are not more wars.

Maciek

Yes, January is bad, but February, it is very bad also. Look! All these people know it too. Every face. Every person, they are so tired now. They want winter to go away. And they are afraid winter begins now. Pale faces, grey faces, empty eyes. Slow feet. There is no hope inside these days, not one gram. But still, the things we all must do. Evanton, it goes to school, to work, to the library and to the dentist. It goes to the shop to buy milk. And I love Ania and she loves her husband and he loves her and she loves me. And there is a baby inside her, and it is not my baby. My head is sore and I feel old.

Today Ania comes, and she runs here in the rain. Rain like the sky has opened. Her hair is very wet – and it makes her face, for a short time, ugly. I notice this. It is the first time I see she is not always beautiful. I am not in love anymore.

'Ania,' I say afterwards, when we are resting, naked. Eyes closed. Her head here, on my chest. 'I love you.'

'I know.'

'But you are careful, yes?'

'Careful? You mean about this? Keeping it secret?'

'Please, you must be very careful.'

'Why? You don't want me to get caught?' She sits up, to say this. She wears the amber necklace from the Cloth Hall.

'No! You must not get caught.'

'You don't want to marry me? You don't love me that much?'

'Stop! I love you, this much I love you. *Kocham cie*! But you don't want to marry me, do you? Look how I live. And your husband, he's someone very ... very important, yes? Schoolteacher. Father of your baby. And he makes good money.'

'You're a teacher too. You teach philosophy!'

'Only in Krakow. And that job, it is not very good money. And anyway, that job is finished. The college, it shuts down that part.'

'So you're jealous then? Jealous of him!'

'No, I'm not. I am not jealous.'

'Liar! You are jealous! You do want to marry me! Confess!'

'Never!' I say. 'I do not!' I really mean this.

'You do!'

Ania laughs – she is so different these days. What happened to my serious careful girl? She never used to laugh like this. She laughs like she's drunk. So I pin her down, and make her stop laughing with kisses.

But I am not in love anymore. I am in something else now. I don't know what.

She is gone already – she never stays long. Sometimes, in a whole week, I will see her for two hours. And it is snowing at last. Inside my caravan, I can hear it falling. Soft quiet thumps on my windows and roof. Marshmallows. Thump, thump, thump. And beyond this, Evanton is quiet. I hear nothing at all. The snow silences it.

I'm out of milk, but I think I'll stay inside. Yes. I have bread and butter. I'll make toast. And when Sam comes, that is what I do. Make toast, and we drink tea with no milk. I put raspberry in the tea. Sam is used to that now.

'So,' says Sam. 'How's the love life?'

'How is my love life? Please, I have a life, and I have some love. But I do not have a love life. My real life has no love in it.'

'Same here. Not yet, anyway. Got any Marmite?' He opens my cupboard doors and pushes jars around.

It's like he's moved in here after all.

Sam

Mum moving out's best thing that's happened since . . . since I met Maciek, actually. Her new place is cool, but I don't go there much. She's not got the internet yet. Anyway, me and Dad, we don't miss her much. We're sound. We've got a routine already, and it doesn't involve talking. None of those stupid endless questions that drove me crazy. Mum always wanting to know every little thing. Who my friends were, what I had for lunch, if I'm wearing warm enough clothes. The truth is, we're both happier with her away. Sure, the house is a tip, and we run out of milk and toilet paper all the time, but so what? It isn't like I'm a kid anymore. Even got the pubes to prove it. Which are very weird things to suddenly have, between you and me. Weird and, well, a relief too. I keep feeling them. Hope I get more soon.

Going to the movies with Roksana today. I've got new jeans, because my old ones are all too short. Got my new jeans, new shirt, and had a haircut yesterday. I am totally psyched. We're taking two buses. From Evanton to Inverness, then out to the retail park. I've got it all sorted. Maybe Burger King after. Or Borders Starbucks. I'm trying very hard to forget the way she is with Jake. Have started to chat to her on Bebo and MSN, under my own name now, but can't quite kill off Jake. The truth is, Jake gets more laughs. She's even hinted that they could meet up one day! Am beginning to wish I'd never created Jake.

On the bus, I'm trying to be sarcastic, like Jake.

'Great day, good thing I brought my sunglasses.'

But Roksana misunderstands.

'What is wrong, Sam? What is this you mean?' We're crossing the Kessock Bridge in a howling gale. Rain is bucketing down.

'Nothing, sorry Roksana.'

'No reason for sorry, Sam.

'Look,' I say, pointing out the window. 'Sometimes you can see dolphins out there.'

Roksana turns to look at the Firth.

'Have you seen the dolphins?' she asks.

'Me? No. Actually.'

'How you are knowing they are there?'

'It's a famous dolphin place. Honest. There's even a car park, and binocular thingies, and a shop and everything.'

Immediately regret saying thingies. What the hell?

'Uh huh,' she says, smiling, but as if she doesn't really care about dolphins at all. As if I haven't given her dolphin earrings. Which she is totally not wearing.

I can't stop looking at her. It's like there's a direct current running between us. I love the way her smile disappears, then bursts out, without any middle ground. I have to keep watching. I don't want to miss anything. Of course I'm getting a stiffie. Who cares. Got my baggie jeans on.

'I like way you speak, Sam. You have a nice melody.'

'You mean my accent? Thanks.'

'You are very welcomed, Sam.'

Her voice is so soft, I have to sit quite close to hear her.

'Want some?' I offer her a sausage roll I bought at the shop. Got hungry waiting for the bus.

'No thank you.'

'Not hungry?'

'No. Yes.' She blushes and says: 'Sam, I will tell you a truth. I do not much like food here.'

I take a bite, and can hardly swallow.

'Crap, isn't it?'

'Maybe is just very much different in Poland.'

'And you like Polish food better?'

'Yes. Yes, of course I like it more! Sam, is more normal for me. I do not understand the thing like vinegar on chips. The bread is not good. And what you call sausage. This is not a sausage,' pointing at my nearly finished sausage roll. 'Where my old home is . . .'

'Where is it?'

'You will not know it. Bielsko-Biala. Near south of country. River running down middle. There is a big castle. Very pretty.'

And then there it is: I want to see this river and this castle, and eat this superior sausage.

'Everything here is not same as Poland, but much is same too.'

'The people? Are we the same?'

'Ummm . . . no, not really. I think that Polish people, we are more . . . act like crazy more? More crying, more loud. Scotland, it is being a soft place. We are not so kind, in Poland. We are mean!'

'Aye, right. So, you think we're a bunch of softies then?'

'Sam, I do not mean it like this.' She puts her hand on my knee, saying this. I am serious. Her actual hand is on my fucking knee. 'Life in Scotland, it is easy here. You do not understand. Not so much poverty here. You need to come to Poland one day. Then you know.'

'Ok.'

'You will go one day?'

'Sure, why not?'

And the more she talks about how great it is, the more Poland begins to take shape in my mind. I know it sounds daft, but I hadn't really thought of it as, like a real place. There really is a world out there, and here is a person to prove it. Like Roksana's a souvenir from it. Proof. The more I think about the world being real, the smaller I feel. I'm shrinking, right here on the bus! But it's ok, because this means that the stuff that happens in Evanton, well, it doesn't really matter. Does it?

It's, like, fuck all.

Cinemas must be the sexiest places on earth. I mean, think of it. It's dark, and you get to sit right close next to a girl for hours. The whole side of my body next to Roksana is tingling. I really wanted to see this film, but I can't follow it at all. All I can think about is how her hand felt, when it brushed mine. Looking for the popcorn, but still. The sexiest touch so far in my life.

Ania

Not a single thought that isn't pornographic. All the time. I am infected with sex. I keep this secret of course. It is like a private film, on continual play mode. I'm in bed, staring at my sleeping husband. Ian MacLeod. Thirty years old, ten stone, five feet ten inches. Teaches English. Likes his steak well done, hates football. Quite unattractive, asleep.

And here am I, next to him: Ania MacLeod, thirty years old, pregnant marriage counsellor. *Pregnant!* Maker of tasty beef casseroles and currently experimenting with adultery.

It doesn't work. These observations, instead of anchoring me, float away. Stupidity keeps demanding my surrender. I try to reclaim some certainties. With my eyes closed, I make a mental list.

Things I Know

1. Pure lust relies on mystery, thrives on unfamiliarity.
2. Routine is death to lust.
3. Therefore, the quicker we establish a pattern, the sooner the lust will fade.

I know I could add to this list, or think of ways to act on this list, but instead I find myself thinking about the changing room at the swimming pool. The way Maciek looked when I returned the favour. Like he was about to cry. Which makes me smile. Here I am, smiling like an idiot.

'*Kocham cie*,' he'd whispered.

'Me too,' I answered, not even knowing what his words meant.

I am full of wonder. I knew about sex, but never realised the truth about lust.

Stop this nonsense Ania! *Right now!*

I have had a spell of hormonal insanity, but I am getting over it now. There is no future with Maciek. I will restrict him to fantasy. Now I am drawing a ring of penicillin around him, forbidding him outside my mind. And then I half dream a dream, as if I am Maciek and myself. I am both of us, the director of my own soft porn film.

She breathes out clouds. I cannot breathe. She pulls me down to her.

'Ania?'

My answering whisper: 'Yes.'

His lips taste of almonds. Unbearably sweet to roll his lips between mine, feel their thickness. I will never get tired of this.

The wetness of her. Look at it – jumps to meet my finger.

No talk. No thought. Pushing, licking, plunging, swooning.

Sounds that are not words.

Foreign words with foreign sounds.

The heat and hardness of him. The heat, the hardness. Jumps when I touch it.

The wetness of her, like wet velvet.

His mouth on me, his tongue greedy.

Then I roll her on her side, and at first she gasps.

He's sliding inside me from behind, hands on my breasts.

Sliding in. At first gently, then not.

Gone.

Lost.

I come silently, just a muffled sigh as I turn to my side. The baby shifts around a little, perhaps a somersault or two, not knowing it is the middle of the night, or that there are things like days and nights. Ian snorts softly, then rolls over, puts an arm around me. Bless.

We are all lost in secret dreams.

Rose

Who would think you could keep a secret in a place like this? But you can. It's not even that hard, because mostly people don't notice stuff that isn't to do with their own lives. Alpin has been here for three weeks, and Harry and Sam don't even know. I was going to tell them, but the right time never seemed to come. I was going to say:

'Hey – told everyone back home about my new place, and you'll never guess who's coming for a holiday. Tommy, James from Lothian, Mum and Dad, and I think Sarah and Alpin might be coming too.'

And then later, I planned to say:

'Disaster! Sarah and Alpin had a huge row. She's pissed off back home, and asked if Alpin could stay up here awhile. Just till she stops wanting to kill him. He brought his laptop, so he's just going to work from the sitting room. Lucky thing about the sofa bed, eh?'

I was even going to suggest Harry take him out for a drink, to cheer him up.

But none of this was said, because . . . well, it just wasn't. I told Lily at work, but she's the only one who knows. I'm busy, I don't see much of the boys, and now it's too late.

Meeting him off the train was romantic as hell. Well, train stations are made for romance, aren't they? A misty, freezing day. Foggy, even on the platform.

He looked better than I remembered, weirdly. Thinner, but then his marriage was over. Older, but I always think it's a good thing when a guy looks older. I don't want him looking at me, and thinking I'm too old for him. I'd changed my clothes about a hundred times that morning. Ended up giving it my best shot. Wore the dress I bought when I turned forty. Decided I was positively vomit-inducing anyway, and he'd get back on the next train. Have I mentioned that I'm quite ugly? Used to be ordinary, but middle age has demoted me to ugly. Very bad timing, with the raging libido.

I saw him before he saw me. I saw him looking for me. His face looked worried. When he saw me, he lit up like a kid. I swear, I adore this man. I could eat him. And I do, as it happens, later. All my worries, all my doubts, all my imagining how love would be gone, were for nothing. I just needed to see him.

He is the man for me. To think I might have gone the rest of my life, and not known this way of being! Such a fluke has made it happen. An accidental kiss in the dark. If I'd aimed properly, been more sober, the kiss would've been just a forgettable goodnight kiss, and I'd be in Leith still, with Harry, and all of my old life. I was so angry all the time.

We don't sleep much at all that first night. We drink too much, of course. We talk about everything, except his wife. I do feel guilty about Sarah. Really, quite a lot. I don't even like to think about the hell she's going through. I wish he'd told me something shitty about her, so I could picture her differently. So I could not feel sorry for her. Almost every time the phone rings, my heart pounds, I'm so sure it's her.

But I could never keep my mouth shut. Especially after a few. About 3am, I blurt:

'Do you regret this?'

'Yeah, I regret this. Falling in love with you has been massively inconvenient.'

'Would you have ever left her if she hadn't busted you?'

'Maybe not. But I'm glad she did.'

'I was so sure you'd see me today and be disappointed.'

'What? Why?'

'Why? Are you insane? There's a million reasons. In case you haven't noticed, I am flaky as hell.'

'Well, there's that.'

'And I have stretch marks. And this belly. And these wrinkles.'

'Aye. Well. I knew about those.'

'And I worried I might not recognise you. Or still feel this way about you.'

'Foolish woman.'

'Well, and there's my track record with relationships. Not brilliant.'

'Horrors!'

'No, I mean it. I'm telling you the truth. I'm not sure I'm any good at relationships. I'm warning you, Alpin: I'm a wee bit fucked up.'

'Let me tell you something true about you.'

'What?'

'You looked lovely at the station today. You are a lovely woman.'

'Oh! Thanks.'

'And you worry too much.'

'Do you think?' I ask worriedly.

'And you're lonely. You've always seemed so very lonely to me.'

I have no answer for this. It makes me feel naked, that he's noticed. And I'm already starkers.

Then he yawns and says: 'Can we go to sleep now, darling? Please. There's a good girl.'

This is how my new life feels: Nervous and happy. Nervously happy. Like one lucky escape after another. Like I am hopping through a field dotted with land mines, and by some miraculous chance my feet land in the right place each time. I am properly breathing, and get this – I actually like myself. I haven't nagged anyone in my nagging voice for ages and ages.

'I feel like you've rescued me,' I whisper to Alpin. We're cuddled up on the sofa. Well, actually he's typing on his laptop, and I am cuddled around him. It's early evening. He's going to cook us a curry later. Harry never cooked; not that I'm comparing, but he didn't.

'True, true,' Alpin mumbles while typing. 'Quite right.'

But then, without warning or sense, I suddenly need Sam. I miss him so much, not even Alpin can kiss it away. It's a physical pain, right here, right in my throat, and here too – in my stomach.

I'll need to explain to Harry and Sam. I'll do that tomorrow. I'll pick up Sam from school, tell him in the car, see if he wants to have dinner with us. Maybe go out for pizza, if that's what he wants. But he's been so distant, so difficult to talk to. Harry's distant too, but that was predictable, even hoped for. Sam has not phoned me once, not asked for anything, hardly visited me, not accused me of abandoning him, or of anything. He's polite and distant, and this hurts like fuck. Because *I know* Sam misses me. He's just being a bloke.

MARCH

Evanton

Snow, when everyone has stopped expecting it. It was so mild the night before, just a light rain. Chapel Street, at 6am, is a soft and smooth white. And every leafless tree is half white, thanks to the northerly breeze. Half a dozen sparrows, three gulls and a sole crow looking thug-like, argue over a black plastic rubbish bag behind The Balconie. The people of Evanton are early risers, most of them, and by 7am, Chapel Street is black again. The ones who are left at home – the mothers with pre-schoolers, the elderly, the unemployed and the wasters, are either sleeping or regarding this snow with surprise. Surprise pleases some of these people, especially those who are grating against their life. It begins to snow again, huge fat flakes, at 10am, and the Evantonians who yearn for fate to change their lives feel their spirits rise. One or two celebrate by playing loud nostalgic songs, and pouring a wee dram into their coffees. And for a moment allow themselves to draw closer to their particular precipice.

We are all drawn to precipices – the point at which change is possible. Who has not vividly imagined leaving their job, their spouse, their town? And then, before leaping, we almost always slip back and sigh with relief, heart pounding. The adrenaline of the imagined leap. But what happens when one leans a millimetre too far over the precipice, in an unguarded moment? Perhaps drunk like Ania was on the Gold Wasser, or hormonally driven like Rose, or simply careless? One can lose one's balance. It happens every day, even in places like Evanton.

By early afternoon the school has closed, and laughing, shrieking children are reappearing in the village. Snow belongs to them. They're unaware of the near escapes of certain parents, and in at least two cases, their toppling. The screams of the topplers are always silent. They have to be.

Maciek

There she is now, with her big belly. There's a lot of snow, and she's slow. I always watch this path in the morning, in case she comes. When I'm an old man, I think this is something I'll remember. Fat Ania, walking up this snowy path to my door. Which she opens without knocking.

'Morning adorable one!' I tell her.

'Good morning, my dearest one,' she says, and smiles.

She takes off her coat and I put the kettle on. Then she stands on tiptoe to take off my hat, and I bow so she can kiss my forehead. Our little ritual. Our empty bottle of Gold Wasser sits on my shelf with a piece of heather she put there. I make the kind of tea she likes, and she drinks it from one of the cups she gives to me. It has poetry on it. Edwin Muir. *Yours, my love, is the right human face.* No, we are not being the way I imagined. This is what we have instead. These things. This way of being.

Later, I rest my head between her magnificent breasts. From here, her belly is a snowy round hill.

'So what is happening today?' I ask her.

She doesn't answer right away. Sighs, like she is annoyed. I can't see her face, only her nipples and belly. I can hear her heart beating. It seems to me, it beats too quickly.

'I'm going to see my Maciek,' she says. 'That's what's happening today.'

'I mean later. After this.'

'I don't want to think about later.'

'Ah, Ania.'

'Do you think love is a reason to hurt people? A good enough reason?' she whispers.

'What's a good enough reason for anything? And do reasons matter in the end, if it all comes good anyway? Let me tell you a story about Poland,' I say. She laughs softly, and my head rocks with her laugh.

'A long time ago, more than three hundred years ago, the capital was in my town. Krakow. The queen falls in love a lot, and her fourth husband is a Swede. He is younger than her, and beautiful. She loves this man, but he does not love her, and he does not love Poland either. He refuses to speak to her in Polish, and she doesn't know Swedish, so they speak to each other in Latin.'

'Latin? People spoke in Latin? You're making this up.'

'No. This is an historical fact. His name is King Zygmunt, and no one in Poland likes him, except the queen, who is in love with him. And he won't even sleep with her.'

'What a mean man. What happened?'

'*Listen.*'

'To what?'

'It's starting to thaw. Listen.' The sound of water dripping and running is loud.

'Pity. Carry on.'

'Anyway, King Zygmunt likes to play with explosives – they are his hobby, in fact. And one day he burns down their castle by accident.'

'Idiot! Did the queen stop loving him then?'

'Not at all. She lets him choose where to build the new castle, thinking it might be down the hill a bit. Closer to her mother. But he chooses a place by looking at a map of Poland and sticks a pin in the very centre.'

'What?'

'He moves the capital of Poland to a sleepy fishing village called Warsaw, just to annoy her.'

'Wow. What did Warsaw think of that?'

'They think it is a joke, of course. It is a terrible reason to choose a capital city.'

'The king was insane.'

'Well, yes, but he also invites Shakespeare to Poland. And painters and musicians. And in the end, Warsaw becomes a fine capital city.'

A pause.

'I'd like to see it one day.'

I lift my head to see her face, because there are tears inside her voice.

She puts her hand on my head, to lower it again, but I can tell she's crying. 'Ania,' I say to her nipples. 'Please.'

'Aye?'

'Do you love your husband?'

'Well, yes.' Her nipples are wonderful nipples. The colour of raspberries.

'Perhaps we should stop, Ania.'

How can I say this again? *Kurwa!* Never planned to say this.

'You don't want to see me again?' Her chest is heaving, but still her hand on my head, keeping it here.

Suddenly, pouring rain. You wouldn't believe how loud rain can be, inside a caravan. You can't think or talk. You can't ignore it.

My throat hurts.

'Rain!' I say. '*Kocham cie*, Ania. Listen to the rain.'

I remember the beginning. I want to marry Ania, after the first time. I have a fantasy of our one baby, our cottage near the river. Now I try to see this river cottage with Ania in it, with us eating breakfast every morning, and it is not so clear. I can't picture us eating Sunday dinner at her parents' house, like she and Ian do. I can't see us pushing a trolley together at Tesco, changing the sheets on the bed, washing dishes. I have great difficulty imagining Ania at a Polish party. Coming to Krakow, with her baby and me. Chatting to Ciotka Agata, eating carp. These are not things I can see. My certainty is gone. Have you ever developed photographs? Sometimes the picture rises up out of the water, sharp and true, as you saw it. Other times, it becomes lost on the way. It's faded, under-exposed, blurred. Even though it seems in focus when you click the shutter. I don't know how this happens. If it's someone's fault.

Sam

It's pissing down, ruining the snow, and there she is. Sitting in her old car. Mum. Why can't she get a decent car, and what the fuck is she doing here? What if someone sees? She hasn't a fucking clue. I could get killed for this. She waves to me, and oh my god, she's holding the bakery bag, which means she's made a special trip to buy a chocolate donut for me. Crap. I stopped liking those donuts years ago.

I ignore her. Head for the bus. Please, Mum: just piss off home. Go!

I'm almost at the bus, when a car pulls up just behind me and it's her. What's she like? Trying to head me off, like this.

I start to run to the bus. I'm getting soaked. And that, no doubt, is the reason she's here. The rain. She thinks I'll melt.

The bus is mental, as usual. Everyone shouting, swearing, throwing shit around. I settle in a seat, forget to not look out the window, and I catch her eyes for a second.

Her whole face lights up with this insane look.

Of course I love her, she's my mum, but she'll have to die. Well, you know. Not really die. I just wish she'd get a life.

At Maciek's later, having a cup of tea, and he says:

'By this way. I am not adulterying anymore.'

'Dumped Mrs MacLeod? Good on ya,' I say.

'Yes. Is being a good thing.'

He totally looks like it's a terrible thing, but I leave it.

'And how is this Polish girlfriend?'

'Her name is Roksana. And she's fine.'

'She has love for you?'

'Nah,' I say. 'She's got lots of boyfriends.'

But I'm only saying this because of Mrs MacLeod and the way Maciek looks. Roksana is definitely in love with me. In class this morning, we got into trouble together, which is practically the same as snogging. We had to stay after class, apologise to Mrs Smith for talking. We've got Biology together too, so we walked together after, slow, and talked about stuff. Mostly she talked, and I listened. Stuff about her parents, who sound even dumber assed than mine. Then we got into trouble again, because we were late for class. Ace day.

Ania

A terrible day. It's over. Can't take it in. I've stopped crying, but I can feel all the tears backing up. Maciek is right of course. I am having a baby with a husband I love. No other solution. It had to end. And I have to be detached now. Be the Marriage Mender.

There's the doorbell.

Help me.

Rose and Harry arrive separately, a few minutes apart. Both have lost weight. They've dressed with care, and I believe Rose has dyed her hair. They look attractive. A bit older, perhaps, around the eyes. Slightly stressed, but also they look in focus. Alert. Poised for newness.

Like an old person reverting to toddler habits, love has a life cycle too. Near death, it returns to the original state. Having said goodbye, Rose and Harry have reverted to individuals primed to be seduced or to seduce.

But I don't feel like that at all. I'm stuck in the middle. I'm still in love, and my lover has said goodbye.

'Well Rose, Harry. You are both looking well. Very well indeed! How are you doing? How are you coping with the new situation? Your separation.'

'Me, I'm alright,' says Harry, with a kind of bravado. I like Harry, he is so lacking in self-pity. 'Me and Sam, we muddle along.' He has not looked at Rose yet.

'Well, I'm not fine,' says Rose, looking at Harry. 'Life is . . . difficult.'

I've seen so many couples sit here in this room. Hundreds. Some couples, I can tell are wrong, and there is nothing between them, no connection. I can assist the severance of their tie, with minimal pain. Like separating Siamese twins surgically, and praying that both will live, because together, they will both certainly die. Other couples, despite little in common, are connected.

I want to tell Harry and Rose: There's probably nothing wrong with you. The cancer is imagined, you're not dying. You're being silly, wantonly destroying what still has a use. You think you're lacking something, but maybe the problem is that you have too much and are greedy. Now you've time for discontent, and you desire intensity. This divorce, if that is what it comes to, might be the product of spoiled boredom. Like peacetime crime. Why sabotage this marriage? Neither of you has someone else. You have a son. Neither of you are drug addicts or physically abusive. You know each other. Wake up, Rose and Harry! Before it is too late!

I want to tell them: Don't listen to me. What do I know? I love my husband and I've a lovely marriage, but I almost tossed it away this morning for a foreigner who wears a trilby and works at Pizza Palace. And I've spent half the day crying, because I miss him.

'I understand that it's very hard. Marriage is hard, and breaking up is hard too. Are you still seeing each other at all, to talk? About Sam? Finances? Your feelings about the future?'

Guilty silence.

'Rose, why don't you start first. Are things going as you hoped they would?'

But Rose cannot speak because she is crying. I pass her the box of tissues I always keep. Of all the unhappy people in the world, the very unhappiest must be the romantics. Life can never live up to their dream. Harry shifts uncomfortably, re-crosses his legs, clears his throat and says:

'This is what you wanted, Rose. For Christ's sake, what do you want now?'

Rose blows her nose, and says:

'I don't know. Sorry. Didn't mean to cry.'

She blows her nose again but neglects to wipe her eyes or cheeks. Her face is shiny with tears. She looks quite pretty this way. Soft.

'I miss Sam.'

'Do you miss Harry?' I ask.

'No.' She cries a bit more, but silently. 'I miss making Sam a cup of tea before school, and picking up his dirty clothes in the bathroom, and him ignoring me with his headphones on.' She laughs then, in a high-pitched hysterical way.

'You should see someone,' says Harry. 'You are cracking up.'

'Yeah, like you would definitely know what craziness was,' she snaps back immediately.

Then she says a very surprised, 'Oh!'

'What is it?' I ask.

'Just realised something else I miss. I miss fighting. With you, Harry. Haven't said fuck off to anyone in ages. No idea how much I miss that.'

'Oh grow up, Rose. This is not a game. You fucked around, then you fucked off. You get what you want every time.'

I've never seen this side of Harry. He is angry. Actually, this is the first time either has sworn in front of me. I guess the gloves are off.

'Fuck off Harry. Just fuck right off.'

'You fuck off, Rose. Fuck off.'

I try to take this seriously, but all I can think of is *fuckfuck-fucking*. Even the word turns me on. I've never noticed what a thrusting word it is. Can a word make you come? I don't see how I'll live the rest of my life, with no Maciek in it. What time is it? Suddenly, my life seems very long indeed.

'Is there anything in particular you two would like to discuss tonight?'

'I have something. Some news,' says Rose. She's blushing. Like she read my thoughts.

'What is it?'

'Remember the man I told you about, the Kiss Man?' she asks me. I don't, but I nod.

'Alpin?' says Harry right away. 'He's here, isn't he? He's left Sarah. I knew it. Knew it! Knew you wouldn't leave me, just to live alone.'

'Aye, well. You were right.'

'Too right.'

'Happy now, then?'

Harry snorts. Laughs an ugly laugh, and says: 'Sure. Delighted. You're happy too, I presume.'

'Oh yes. Very.'

'So Rose,' I interject, wondering what to say next. I am surprised. She fooled me.

'You'll be wanting a divorce, then,' says Harry. He doesn't wait for an answer. 'You've got it, Rose,' he says quietly. 'You win.'

And he stands up and leaves, though there is still thirty-five minutes to go.

Rose blows her nose.

'Sorry, Ania. Really, I wanted to tell him before.'

'Yes. It can be quite frightening to say these things.'

She stands up too, puts on her coat.

After she's gone, I find the appointment book and cross off their appointments. Then I turn on my phone, wait a minute. Nothing. I wait another minute, will him to ring or text. Promise myself that if he does not, then I will not either. Then I scroll to his name in the contact list and delete it. Easy!

Then I go to my inbox, open his last email, save the number, add his name, and breathe again.

Rose

Living with Alpin is as easy as breathing. As a mince and tattie day. He's just so damn pleasant to be with. Easy to talk to, easy to please, easy to love. But it does seem a little odd that he's fallen into this other life so easily. I picture the house he's left, and imagine chaos and sadness. His kids maybe going back to sucking their thumbs and wetting the bed, while his wife weeps over the kitchen sink. He was happy in his marriage all those years, and a minute after leaving it, he's happy with me. It occurs to me that Alpin is a happy-natured person, who doesn't particularly need me to be happy. It almost seems unnatural that he is so happy, so relaxed.

Probably I'm just not used to anything being easy and pleasant; makes me slightly nervous. I am braced for upset. For criticism and contradiction.

It's been almost a month now, and I'm trying to relax into it, not feel I'm the hostess all the time, not make a fuss of him being here. It is his house too, I want him to feel free to do whatever he wants, and it needn't be with me every damn minute. And to tell the truth, it's a bit hard to be cranky around someone who never gets cranky. So I head into town to see if there's anything new in Monsoon. And there's Harry walking across Falcon Square, with a red-haired woman. Holding hands. Laughing. The woman looks about thirty, and she's laughing too.

I freeze and stare, heart pounding, then dash into Laura Ashley, even though I hate Laura Ashley. Monsoon would be too dangerous, as that's where Harry and his handholding woman are heading. Why isn't Harry at work? He normally works Saturdays. More to the point, why isn't Harry alone and unable to get over me? Fuck sake, it's only been a week since I told him about Alpin.

After a while of acting like I care about floral prints, I leave Laura Ashley, and my first impulse is to talk to Sam. It's unbearable that my only child is a stranger to me. Why should Harry get the closeness of our son, plus a girlfriend? In Starbucks, I burn my tongue on the coffee and ring Sam's number. The café is noisy and crowded. Everyone has carrier bags, and it also seems like they are all with someone. Someone asks if I need the other chair at my table, and when they take it, I notice I'm the only woman sitting on her own. Sam's number rings, and I'm relieved. Sometimes he turns it off. I wait for his voice, when the ringing is cut off. He'll have known it was me. Has Sam hung up on me? I blush, alone at my table with my scorched tongue, and I try Sam's number again. This time I get voice mail. He's turned his phone off.

Starbucks is relentlessly happy. I want to go home to Alpin. I need to get into bed with him, and stay there for a long time. With twelve bottles of wine.

But when I get home, Alpin is not there and there's no note. Well, we never agreed to leave each other notes, so it's no big deal. We don't really have rules yet.

I walk to Kiltearn Beach, walk around the churchyard – old graves are so cheering, don't you think? I stop by the Polish graves, the soldiers from World War II, and I think of Ania's dad. What different lives we all have. And what short lives.

So Harry doesn't miss me and never cared about making me happy. So Alpin is happy no matter what, would never understand the way I occasionally am not. So Sam doesn't need me, and I need him.

So what? This is my life. I try repeating it a few more times.

Harry doesn't need me, Alpin doesn't need me, Sam doesn't need me.

Who really needs me? *Really.* No one.

At first this sounds like a terrible fact. But suddenly, right there, by the grave of a man called Donald Angus McDonald, who died in 1822, aged forty-seven, and whose wife strongly recommended him for a front row seat in Heaven, my heart soars. It literally does. I feel like I've just lost a stone. My life is not good or bad; it's my life. I wonder what will happen next? I feel like I did on the first day of secondary school, everything new and strange. Walking in through the huge front doors and brushing shoulders with tall boys I didn't know the names of yet, the air full of promise.

APRIL

Evanton

It is freezing still, most days, until it is not, and one evening there is a sudden warming of air at dusk. No one removes their jackets for this air. They are warm, but too immersed still in winter. Middle-aged women blame their hormones. Babies in prams arch their backs and try to squirm out of their blankets, but their mothers cover them up quickly. Boys don't wear jackets anyway, mostly, but are too worried about being the most daring on the skateboard or bike or kicking the footie, to notice the warm air. Thirteen-year-old girls don't notice either. Instead, they find themselves breaking into a skipping run down Chapel Street, for no good reason at all. Their giggles alert the boys, who drop their footballs and bikes and skateboards, and find themselves grouping by the bus shelter, claiming this territory for the first time. Bikes are mounted, and ridden with the front wheel off the ground. Lipstick is over-applied. Cigarettes are lit and disgust concealed.

Up on Ben Wyvis, snow-melt washes the stony mountain. Oblivious to Evantonians and all their preoccupations, the world is turning; it has never stopped.

Of course life is change and chance all the time, but spring seems to celebrate this as if it owns change and chance. Anything at all might happen. From the fluke car coming onto the pavement just in time to run you down as you race late for work, to the rogue sperm that makes its goal in forty-five-year-old Edith-without-hope, or sixteen-year-old Chloe. From a girl from Bielsko-Bialo falling in love with a fourteen-year-old boy from Leith, to a man from Krakow saying goodbye to a woman he thinks he doesn't love anymore.

Maciek

I brush my teeth and she is not here. I drink my tea and she is not here. Every morning, she does not walk up the path to my door. Look! No Ania. In this bed, no Ania! Her absence, it is a quiet, deflated thing. It makes the days too long. My days are empty of Ania, but my head is full of her.

Spierdolilem!

On and on and on.

I tell myself do not text, then watch myself text:

pls come. Need u.

Kurwa! Then I send another text:

XXX hurry

I am not in love with Ania. I'm in worse trouble than being in love.

Sam

I'm fifteen today. Like that makes a difference. Happy birthday, a hundred years! That's how Maciek says happy birthday. *Boab.*

They want to give me a party next Saturday. Mum and Dad, pretending they're friends, in front of me. Smiling like morons. Well, more Mum smiling. Dad actually has the good sense to look a bit embarrassed.

'Whatever you like, son,' he says.

'Invite all your friends!' says Mum.

Then Mum gives me this look, and asks if I have friends. She's no fucking clue. Course I've got some friends now. No idea where they live. Damn sure I don't want them anywhere near this house for a birthday party. Mum would probably bake a lopsided cake with some stupid design on it, like a football or a tractor or maybe even Shrek, for fuck sake. There'd be balloons everywhere, knowing her, and even games.

'No thanks,' I say. 'Don't want a party, ok?'

So she gives me £50 and the new jeans I wanted, wrapped in birthday paper, and goes back to her own house, where he is. Alpin. Her boyfriend. Very fucking weird to say that out loud. Me and Dad watch the footie. Not crazy about football, to be honest. But it's habit, and besides, don't know how to tell Dad. He's obsessed with it.

So there we are, sitting in front of the telly, and Dad gets so excited, he actually shouts and swears, and I fetch him more beer so he doesn't have to miss anything.

Dad's different, since Mum left. He's nicer, actually. Hardly ever shouts, or even asks me to tidy up. Actually, now I think of it, Mum is nicer too. Still a pain, but basically there are no rules anymore. And all they do is ask how I am and buy me shit. All this niceness should be good news, but it's not. It's too weird.

After the game, which I have not really watched at all, me and Dad get an Indian, which we have to re-heat. Tastes a bit off, to tell the truth, but I don't say. Very glad the new girlfriend isn't here. She's ok, but it's hard to feel at home, when she's here too. When Dad sings me happy birthday, I notice he's looking thinner and older. It's boab, seeing him like that.

On MSN, I check out Jake's site, and a second later, she's chatting to him. Roksana saying hi to Jake. What's she doing, checking him out? She's got her webcam on, and I can see she's got on the dolphin earrings. This is like, the crappest birthday ever. Jake, being a fake person, can't have a webcam. I can watch her, but all she can see is Jake's photo.

<Nice earrings,> I message as Jake.

<Thanks,> she smiles and touches them. She hardly ever smiles, how's Jake getting that smile?

<Where'd u get them?> I ask before I can stop myself. Jake would never ask stuff like that.

She notices. Fuck. And says:

<Why?>

<Was looking for a pair for my sister.> I'm quite proud, for thinking of this so quick, like. It's just what Jake would say. I'm in his skin now. I can hardly remember being that other ned.

<Dunno. New Look? A prezzie, can't remember who.>

This is wrong on so many levels, I lose the Jake mindset and just sit there.

<U still there?> she asks.

New Look? Nothing in New Look costs more than 50p, for fuck sake.

<Jake?>

Can't remember *who* the prezzie was from?

It's only half nine, so I head to Maciek's. I want to let Maciek know I'm fifteen now. He might want to give me a present. He hasn't thanked me for the Christmas present yet, but this'll remind him.

Some pricks spray-painted words on Maciek's caravan, on the top part, which is white. They say: Feck off and die polak. It's black paint, and dripping in places, though it's dry now. I wonder if it was Kyle and that lot. Someone spray-painted some swears in the bus shelter last week, and before that, the post office. I know not everyone likes Maciek. On account of him being Polish. But it seems a bit much, wanting him to die. I decide to offer to paint over it, but the door's locked.

Then I hear something. Like someone's hurt, inside. Very weird that the door is locked, if he's home.

'Maciek! Are you alright? It's me. Sam.'

There's no answer, and I am about break open the door and rescue Maciek, when I hear a woman laughing inside. Then Maciek is laughing too, and he calls out:

'I am fine Sam! Come back later!'

So much for ending it with Mrs MacLeod.

'Oh feck off and die,' I say. But he can't hear me. Anyway, I don't mean it. I mean, I know he's thirty-seven, but Maciek seems more like a kid than me. She better not screw him around. *Women.*

Ania

What kind of woman am I? I'm due next month, and hardly think of this baby at all. I look at my body in the mirror after my shower and rub cream on my belly. Assume it will come, the famous maternal instinct. I know the baby is real, of course, but it doesn't feel real. All my life, I've watched the world from a distance, and never more so than now.

I am a disgrace to the profession of marriage counselling. You must resign tomorrow, I tell myself. Then I get dressed, a maternity dress with a low neckline. Still in love with my own cleavage. I tell myself Maciek will not be home, he will be at work, slicing pizzas, but I drive by his caravan anyway. And then, because suddenly there is nothing inside my head but a huge yearning, I stop the car anyway, and sit on the bench in front of his caravan.

My breasts rub against my dress in their new way, and I lean back and let my eyes close momentarily. Give in to the spring sun, as thin as it is; I feel I need it. My face drinks it in, and I let my thoughts go where they will. But they are not thoughts at all. I hear footsteps and I know they are his. I keep my eyes shut. Everything is easy now he is here. Everything is false, everything is work, except being right here.

'Do you miss Poland?' I ask Maciek later, as I am dressing again.

'Of course,' he says. He is not dressing, just laying there. He smells like . . . like a man who has just had sex.

'Your aunt? Your cousins and friends?'

'Yes, I sometimes miss them. And I miss the food. And the trams and the streets and the cabarets.'

I'm hurt that he misses anything. I should be enough compensation.

'Also, I miss the seasons.'

'We have seasons,' I say petulantly, pulling on my jeans. The stretchy elastic bit pulls to just under my breasts. I look like Mrs Humpty Dumpty.

'Your seasons are not good. Not like Polish seasons.'

'Oh.'

'And I miss talking in Polish, Ania.'

'Oh.'

'Ania, come here. Stop being sad.'

We are always telling each other what extraordinary lovers we each are. But the truth is, we are only ordinary lovers. When we touch, we are saying I love you.

The next day, we meet again.

'Maciek,' I say. 'We've got to stop this. Really stop, this time. Say goodbye.' The words sound melodramatic, sitting here in Tesco café. We are surrounded by a cacophony of human noise and shifting merchandise.

'Ania,' he says, reaching for my hands under the table. 'I want you to be having happiness, always. Happiness.' He says happiness as if it is three words, all of them full to the brim with tenderness.

'By next month there'll be a baby, Maciek.'

'I know this,' he says, with his intelligent sad smile. 'It is not a thing you can hide.'

'I can't see how there is room for a baby in this. There isn't.'

'There is room now, and look! He, or maybe she, is already taking up space.'

The baby is dancing like mad, while we talk.

'Not the same, Maciek, and you know it. It will never be the same.'

'Alright,' he says, tilting his head sideways. His hat is on the table between us. I remember our first meeting here. At that table over there. 'We can be ended. Again.'

'Maciek, it's best. You'll be alright. Won't you?'

He sighs and shrugs. Not in a self-pitying way at all. Maciek's face is as close as a man's face can get to a woman's face, and still be manly. I want to stroke his cheeks, his forehead, I want to sweep his hair back and suck his ear lobe.

'No, I am not alright. Do you think I am alright with not seeing you again?'

'But Maciek, what can we do?'

'We can leave here. You and me.'

'And go where?'

'Anywhere. Poland.'

'But this baby.'

'I love this baby already. And we have more, later.'

I am smiling, despite myself.

'Twenty-five more babies!' He is smiling now too.

His hands have found my hands under the table. They are pouring warmth into me. Our hands are nestled damply under my belly, which now sits on my lap. I can feel myself blush – to be holding hands in the Tesco café with a man not my husband. I am not a brave woman after all. I am a very fat in-love woman.

'And what would we do in Poland, Maciek? I don't even speak Polish.'

He shrugs.

'What would we do?'

'What we would do anywhere. We would live,' he said.

What will become of us? I have no idea.

What a curious sensation, uncertainty. Once, a long time ago, on my way home from somewhere, I boarded the wrong train. Right platform, wrong time. I realised it at the first stop, which was not the one I expected. I didn't know where the train was going. There was no one else in the carriage to ask, and I couldn't stop the train. It was out of my control, and briefly exhilarating.

But of course, later when I'm in the bath, I realise that's just rubbish. I make choices. We all do. There are only temporary states of genuine freedom from responsibility. When the ticket conductor asked for my ticket, I simply told him I was on the wrong train, and he explained what to do. I got home fine.

Things You Cannot Choose

1. To avoid natural disasters. Weather. Earthquakes.
2. To avoid man-made disasters. War. Car accidents.
3. To avoid getting lost sometimes. Boarding wrong trains.
4. Other people's actions. A thief. A benefactor.
5. Your family. Parents, siblings, children. They are themselves.
6. Who you fall in love with.
7. Unplanned pregnancy.
8. To avoid illness always. Cancer doesn't wait to be invited. Strokes are never chosen.
9. Winning lottery numbers. Well, not often.

Things You Can Choose

1. What clothes to wear.
2. What to eat and drink.
3. Where to live, and how to live. Sloppy or tidy.
4. Whether to drink alcohol, take drugs.
5. How you act towards people. People you love, and people you do not like.
6. How you react to experiences you have no control over. Like house fires, and falling in love.
7. What names to give your children.

You may not be able to choose the experience, but you can choose how to react to it.

Rose

I choose a Bart Simpson Easter egg for Sam. Then because it is a two-for-one sale, I choose another one for Alpin, though I am not even sure he likes chocolate. I put camembert, oatcakes, red wine, Parma ham and French bread in my basket. I used to feel jealous of women who had baskets like this.

Do I still feel married to Harry? Aye, I do. Probably my bad luck to end up being one of those sad cases who can't quite disconnect from the dad of their kids. And there in the queue is that very same man. The one I used to wake up with every day, mostly with great indifference, and whom I still consider my property. Even though I have my happy Alpin and Harry has a big-boobed redhead. Even though I dislike him intensely. I'm not a list maker, but if I was, I'm pretty sure the list of reasons Harry pisses me off would be so long, it'd go out the door. All I have to do is think of him, and my stomach clenches, all ready for shouting. Lazy, selfish, smug, small-minded, small-hearted, petty man. Did I mention selfish already?

'Hello,' says Harry. Formally.

'Hello,' I say, equally cool. 'How are you?'

'I'm fine, how are you?'

'Fine.'

'Lovely spring weather,' I say. Suddenly need him to miss me. Fuck! I blame the big-boobed one.

'Yes. Bound to be some lambing snows though.'

'That's what I hear too.'

'Sam alright?'

'Sure, he's fine.'

'I worry.'

'No need.'

And off we go, me to my tidy cottage and Alpin, and Harry to our old messy house on Camden Street. Like the two dogs in the P.D. Eastman story that Sam used to love. *Go, Dog. Go!* The girl dog keeps asking the boy dog if he likes her new hat, and he keeps saying no, and then they both wave bye-bye and ride their bikes in opposite directions. Bastard!

But then, as I pull up to my new house, my whitewashed cottage with daffodils, it's alright. Maybe it's this warm breeze, or maybe it's the sight of Alpin's clothes hanging on the line. He's made an amazing lasagne. I don't tell him what a lasagne day means at Kiltearn Primary. The evening is so light, we take a walk after dinner and head down the beach, walk over the old bridge, and up the river. I want to see these bluebells everyone in Evanton keeps going on about, hope they are out. And there they are – and, well, there is no way to describe them un-naffly. Why should something so beautiful make me sad? I wish I was a writer some days. Then I could talk about the bluebell woods without sounding like a twat.

On the way home, Alpin tells me:

'Sarah rang.'

There's been nothing in the day, nothing in the lasagne to indicate this. I keep walking and act normal.

'Did she? What did she say?'

'She wants me to come home.'

'She's forgiven you?' I drop his hand at this point. Move some distance.

'She needs me to come back.'

'And are you?' Though I know the answer. Have a temporary understanding of suicides. And murderers.

Later, he lights a fire, despite me saying why bother. He opens a bottle of expensive port. Which I have been equally indifferent to, but am drinking. He is not a bad man. But a dangerous man to love. I see that now.

'Don't be angry Rose.'

'I'm not,' I say angrily. 'When are you leaving?'

'Soon.'

'Why not tomorrow morning?'

'Aye. Good idea. Can you take me to the train station?'

'No.'

'Thought not. Sorry. Stupid idea.'

Then later, because there is no other place to sleep, and because, despite everything, I still have hope, I crawl drunkenly into bed with him. I think to myself: Here is Rose, fifty years old. Bit overweight, bit past it and saggy, crawling drunkenly into bed with the lover who has rejected her. I bet she gives him a blow job anyway. Self-loathing is never far away. It doesn't need summoning.

'Oh Rose, darling, please don't. You don't need to.'

'I want to.'

'I don't deserve you.'

'Too bloody true.'

'Crap. I am the luckiest man alive.'

'How can you be so bloody happy about everything?'

'I don't know. Low IQ?'

And then, because I'm never going to see him again, and I am drunk and really needing to know, I ask:

'What am I going to do now?'

I hate myself even more now, because tears have found their insidious traitorous fucking way to my voice.

'Oh Rose.'

He pulls me up, puts his hands on my head, which has landed on his fabulous chest. Strokes me. He has no idea what this does to me. Tears are just pouring now.

'Rose, darling. You'll be fine. You'll do what you always do.'

'What's that?'

'Why, you'll keep living your life, Rose,' he says in his bedtime story voice. 'You'll comb your hair, put on your prettiest clothes. Go to work, and meet your friends later. Take walks, read books. You'll go to movies, and pubs and maybe Majorca in the summer. You'll drink expensive wine, and be glad I'm not with you, being boringly happy.'

In the morning, I don't get up with him. He brings me a cup of tea, which I do not drink. I watch him pack. It doesn't take long. His packed bag, I notice, is quite small. As if he'd never intended staying long.

'Sorry, Rose. Truly, I never meant to hurt you.'

'Aye. Well.'

He tries to kiss me goodbye on my mouth, but I swerve my face, so he kisses my cheek instead. Then he sighs, like I've let *him* down, and says:

'Try not to be bitter.'

'Try not to be an arsehole,' I say.

Maciek

I always try to keep warm. My home, my caravan, it's still cold, even though it's not winter anymore. And there is the smell of Calor gas, always. I go to Mr McKenzie and tell him again.

'Tighten the bottle,' he says. 'You comprende? The big orange bottle outside the caravan. Screw the top down tight.' He says these words very loud, as if I cannot hear, and he shows me with his hands too. Like this. Then he just gets his angry look again, like he's in the middle of some very important thing and I stop him.

'Yes,' I say. 'Thank you.'

Right now, I don't know if I miss Ania. This is the truth. I came to Scotland to escape being sad. But it's like the grease spot you try to paint over. The blue-tack spot. No good! Each time, the spot, it comes back. My blues are a blue-tack spot. And I am a piece of pepperoni.

I go to work, and Sam says right away:

'Fucking hell, you look like death Maciek. What's up?'

I laugh before I speak. Sam can do this. 'Nothing,' I lie. 'Nothing is up.'

'Aye, right. What is it, mate? Tell me.'

Pizza Palace is not open yet. We are slicing the onions, peppers. Grating cheese.

'Sam, it is nothing, really. I am tired.'

'Is it her? Has she dumped you again? Bitch.'

'We both know. Ania and me. It is not possible.'

'Well, duh. She shouldn't have shagged you in the first place. Greedy cow.'

'Sam, don't be like this about Ania. It is my idea, not her idea. At the start.'

'Well, still. I bet she's not looking totally fucked like you.'

'I hope not. I don't want her to be fucked.'

'Unless it's by you, right?'

'Sam! Stop this, alright?'

'Well, stop feeling so sorry for yourself. So it didn't pan out. Big deal. She's only a woman. Get over it! Suck it up, mate.'

'Yes. Please, I wish it was easy to suck, like you say. But tell me about your girlfriend. How is she? Is she in love with you yet?'

'Oh yeah. Totally in love with me. Not.'

'Ah Sam. What happens to this Polish girl? She sounds very nice.'

'Nah. She's just normal nice. Anyway, I don't care. She can go wank herself.'

Later, when I am making king-sized pepperoni for a policewoman, Sam suddenly says:

'Maciek! I've got it! Go home.'

'But the shop doesn't close till nine.'

'I mean Poland, you idiot. You're a miserable git here. No offence, but what are you doing in Scotland, anyway?'

I think of Marja. And Ciotka Agata. Then I think of the little green room at my favourite café, and the little tables with cloths, and clear as this pepperoni, I see myself sitting there. Drinking vodka, with cherries.

Sam

Where's Maciek? He needs to know about this fight at school. He would definitely appreciate it. Where is he? I need to tell him.

At break, everyone's just hanging, and Kyle, who is basically a dick like Jake now I think of it, gets challenged by Euan Munro from Strath. It's been coming for a long time. Kyle's been calling Euan a fag and shit like that since first year. I'm just heading to the high street for lunch, when I hear:

'Fight! Kyle and Euan Munro from Strath.' Poor sod – there's so many of them, he never just gets called Euan, or even Euan Munro.

So I'm there right away, of course. Everyone is. Euan has his people behind him. All the Straths. All Kyle's got is Lee and Malcolm.

This is going to be beast.

Euan gives his jacket to his friend. Kyle pulls off his jumper. I take off my jumper, and so do some others. A real fight, we're thinking. Like it never happens at Dingwall, but you never know. Euan and Kyle call each other fags and cunts for about thirty seconds. Then they say:

'Your mum.'

'*Your* mum!'

And they're off. Fists everywhere, no skill at all, hardly any blood. Kyle looks like he's about to cry, then he just flies and punches Euan on the nose, and he's down. Euan crumbles to the grass, Kyle starts to kick him like he's going to kill him, Euan holds his balls and says *fuck* a lot, Euan's people start pulling Kyle off Euan, then Lee and Malcolm, like, wake up and start pulling everyone off Kyle.

The whole thing lasts about forty seconds. Then Mr Taylor who teaches P.E. just waltzes up, all calm like, and says:

'That's enough, boys.'

He doesn't even need to touch anyone.

Kyle and Euan stop.

'Didn't start it,' mumbles Euan.

'Wasn't me,' says Kyle.

That's boab. It just is.

Where is Maciek?

Maybe he's taken my advice and gone back to Poland. That would be boab too.

Ania

Where is Maciek? He's not been at the swimming pool, or the Tesco café, or Pizza Palace.

I hope he's just home, nursing a cold. Not depressed. I've been depressed, and dislocated, but I'm getting better. It feels like I've come back home after a long absence. I'm drinking camomile tea and listening to Pavarotti sing 'Ave Maria'. This calms me. Easter Sunday in a few days, and I'll go to early Mass with Dad, and have Easter breakfast at their house. Ian will sleep in, and I'll wake him when I return, with a kiss. It turns out I don't know much about love, but I've always understood the importance of gestures. I bought Ian a special Easter present. A ring. A ring is symbolic, and I need to commit to him again. It has a green stone, actually green amber from Poland. It's rare, and I will need to tell him this, or he'll not fully appreciate it. It's also symbolic because I want to introduce him to the Polish in me. And I want to use my maiden name again, as a middle name. I am, I have always been, Ania Zamoyski.

I've been foolish. He doesn't know about Maciek, but I'm in his debt for allowing me Maciek. I think he understands the new power shift. He hardly ever looks at me these days. And he never asks how I am. He asks how the baby is. I always say fine. And it is. I love the way my stomach is so solid now. Like a shelf. I will love this baby. I will. I'll probably have another one, in about two years. And one day I will celebrate a golden anniversary with Ian, and these children I have not met yet. I guess I haven't met the people myself and Ian will be then, either.

I worry about Maciek, of course. Now I'm recovering, I see that it's him, not me, who is vulnerable. Who is innocent.

I have a Relate appointment tonight. A couple who were delighted when I told them Rose and Harry cancelled. I hardly have the heart for it, but my long experience means I can act on automatic. Like an actress who can take to the stage minutes after the portentous telegram. I go up the stairs to my counselling room and wait for the bell to ring.

And when I ask for help, I narrow my plea.

Help me be careful with people, I pray.

We are all so fragile, really.

EASTER SUNDAY

Evanton

A classically joyous morning, guaranteed to send any depressives over the edge. Blue sky, birdsong, blossoms. The lot.

Rose falls asleep finally at 3:40, and wakes at 6:15. Feeling disoriented. Terrified. The memory of Alpin is already ephemeral. His kisses, his taste, his voice: a deep dream, without much aftermath. She makes herself a cup of tea. Decides to give the Open University a whirl. A literature course. What has she got to lose? She's not young, but she's only going to get older. Contemplates the Bart Simpson Easter egg, which she'd bought for Alpin, sitting on her table, then puts on her jacket and goes out. In the car, she puts the CD on again. Eva Cassidy sings 'It Doesn't Matter Anymore'; heartbreak delivered in the lightest of heartbreaking voices. She isn't thinking of Alpin. Rose and Harry have a song after all! But it's a break-up song, and Harry doesn't know it.

The house seems asleep when she arrives, so she just leaves the egg on the table. She's given Sam his egg, but she assumes he's already eaten it. She doesn't know why she's here, in the house she chose to leave. She's glad the door was unlocked, but now she feels nervous. An intruder! Everywhere she looks, there are things that remind her of her past. The photo of Sam as a toddler, the vase her mum gave her twenty years ago. But there might be a strange woman in her bed. Another woman, curled up to the husband she tossed away. She leaves and drives to Kiltearn Beach, where the golden light and calm shimmering firth makes her cry, of course. Crying seems to be her new hobby. Some swans glide by, and she has to drop to her knees and howl. It is early, not quite 8:00. No one sees her.

Harry is not asleep and hears her leave. He's very glad Susan didn't waken. But he'll need to wake her up soon. He prefers to spend his Sundays alone with his son, even if they don't really talk. In any case, on any day he finds it tiring when she stays too long in his house. He can't stop feeling like she is company he must entertain. Be a host to. She's hot, and it's a laugh, and it's revenge, but it is not relaxing. He realises he'll need to work on this. Get to know her. That time will turn Susan into a relaxing presence. That his life will need some conscious input for the foreseeable future, if he doesn't want to sleep alone. This thought makes him yawn.

Ania is awake; the baby already breaks her night's sleep, and she is tired. Ian is asleep, and she watches him for a while. It is true, he is the right man for her. They want the same things. They do wholesome things together, like gardening and shopping. They have similar backgrounds. Just because he cannot kiss like Maciek, doesn't mean anything. He is her husband. He is a good man. She watches this man and is filled with – not love particularly, but gratitude. Maybe there's no difference.

Maciek is awake too, remembering Easter Mass at home. The Easter breakfast food sitting in the pantry. The mazurek*, with a lace cloth to keep it from flies. It's light outside his caravan, and dogs bark dog messages to each other. Rooks shout: get out of bed! Now! Maciek wants Ania; it's a deep and pure wanting, and without the distractions of the day yet, it hurts. He tortures himself by picturing all the Evanton couples, still asleep in warm beds, legs and arms casually tangled. Farting and snoring, and taking each other for granted. Maybe waking and scolding each other. Looking ugly and not caring and saying: Stop stinking the bed out! Did you set the alarm like I said? Stop hogging all the quilt! Yawning and scratching, complaining about the weather and all the things that do not matter and fill up lives. The special brand of coffee that he always forgets to buy. The way she spends too much on shoes. All I want is to be like this, thinks Maciek. To have some woman say,* to have Ania say: *Maciek! You bought the wrong coffee again! I miss this nagging woman, he whines to himself, but in this moment of abject self-pity, he falls into a happy dream.*

Sam sits on the steps of Maciek's caravan ten minutes later. He really needs to talk to him. No one answered his knock and the door is locked, which means Maciek is still asleep. Like his mother, Sam did not sleep well, and is feeling very tense. As if this sun is dangerous, must be guarded against. Battled till clouds come and reassert the rightful dim. But it isn't just the sun; it's the dance, last Friday, and Roksana. The way her waist felt when he put his hands on it, for that dance. Then Kyle asking her to dance, and the way she hardly looked for Sam the rest of the night. Topped off by his mum picking him up, with a bright smile and a bag of cookies, and a million mum questions. The whole night sucked.

'Fine, fine, fine, the dance was fuckin' fine!' he screamed at her, finally. She shut up then, but made a lot of distressing swallowing sounds, like she wanted to cry. Worst night in his life. A night that will take five-and-half years to lose the sting of.

He takes out his box of matches and lights a cigarette. A man needs a vice, after all. At least till he gets some facial hair. Ennui suddenly swamps him. He starts lighting matches out of boredom and flicking them to see how far they can stay alight. Tufts of grass sizzle, but not for long. The dew is still there. Four matches, five, ten. Then he loses concentration, and stops looking where he is flicking them.

For no particular reason, or perhaps because there has recently been murder in his heart, Sam suddenly remembers that he will die one day. As will his mum and dad and even Maciek. Not only that, but after he is dead, he will never be alive again. The world will be here, Evanton will be here, and Dingwall Academy and the bus shelter, but he will not be here. How does this make him feel? He immediately fills with homesickness, though he interprets it as stomach ache. He is homesick for his childhood, where thoughts of death never entered.

He tells himself he needs some breakfast, and he thinks of the Bart Simpson egg his mother gave him. He has not eaten it. It is sitting on his desk. He flicks one more lit match, shoves the empty box in his pocket and heads home.

He is half way to the road when it happens. An explosion so loud, at first it has no sound. Only the air pushing Sam to the ground. Then an echoing roar.

Rose

There's an odd fizzing sound in my ears. Can shock cause this? The police phoned Harry, who phoned me, and now we are both in his car, on our way to Raigmore Hospital. We are sitting as far from each other as possible. Harry blames it all on me, of course.

'Fuck off! How should I know what he was doing there?' I tell him. It's the old familiar anger. God, despite everything, it is comforting to be angry at Harry. 'Why wasn't he in bed, at home? Did you know he wasn't home?'

'For fuck sake Rose, I was asleep! It wasn't even eight.'

'What the fuck was he doing there?'

'How the fuck would I know?'

We basically spit at each other for a few more minutes, then calm down.

'I don't understand any of it,' I admit. 'What caused the explosion?'

'No idea. Pretty sure no one lives there anyway.'

We get there, do the whole car park thing. Like a fucking nightmare, the same slow motion. Looking for a space to park, row after row is full, and all I want to do is fuck the car, just leave it, doors open, in the middle of the fucking road. Out of my way! I want to scream at everything and everyone between me and Sam.

'Your son suffered shock, and is experiencing some deafness and bruising, but he'll be fine,' the doctor is saying. 'We've given him something to help him sleep.'

Sam lies on the bed between us, seemingly unconscious. His face looks young, far younger than fifteen. The Mickey Mouse wallpaper doesn't help.

'When can we take him home?'

'We'll want to keep him overnight for observation, but you can stay here if you like. We have a family room.'

'I'll stay,' I say, without looking at Harry. He doesn't matter right now, anyway. He can do whatever he likes. He can have four big-breasted girlfriends. I am not interested.

'I'll stay with Sam,' says Harry, a second after I say it, so Harry finishes his sentence last. Lamely.

We glare at each other.

'I believe the police are wanting a word,' says the doctor, cautiously. 'They want to speak to Sam when he's rested, and in the meantime, they've asked for you to ring them.'

'The police?'

'Is Sam a witness to something?'

'They'll just want to talk to him about it.'

'No one else was hurt, were they?'

The doctor gives us an odd look, then says: 'The police can answer your questions.'

'Maybe they think Sam caused it.'

'Here's the number. You can use the phone in reception.'

We're alone in the waiting room, an ugly hard room, when the police arrive. Two young men, with wholesome faces. We both respond the way we acted around Ania at the start. We gush. But these men are not sensitive to gush.

'We've reason to believe the explosion was caused by your son.'

'What?'

'No! How?'

'It may not have been intentional, but firemen have discovered evidence that it was caused by a leaking gas pipe, leading to the caravan. The gas may have been accumulating under the caravan, and your son had an empty box of matches in his pocket.'

'I'm sure Sam would never do such a thing. Why would he?'

'We're not accusing anyone of anything just now. There are lots of possibilities. We're trying to eliminate possibilities. Was your son acquainted with the tenant of the caravan?'

'No. Not that I know of.'

'Was someone in the caravan?'

And finally, because we forget momentarily everything except now, we draw closer. As if the explosion, in some weird time-lapsed way, has pushed us as well. As if a vacuum has sucked us into it. My ears fizz even louder. After the policemen go and before we can begin to really think, Harry sighs. Puts both hands on my shoulders, looks me in the eyes and asks:

'Rose, do you love me? At all?'

What?

'Love you? I don't even like you!'

'Good. Just thought I'd check.'

He drops his hands, turns and marches out of the ugly room.

'Wait! Harry!' He doesn't wait, so I have to chase after him as he heads for the lift, and I stumble because my eyes are full of fucking *fucking* tears, and no, I do not give a fuck who sees me.

'Wait for me! What's love got to do with anything, Harry?'

I grab his hand and hold it. Squeeze it. And miracle of fucking miracles, a trickle of electricity travels from my hand to his. I can see the second it arrives. Despite me, despite him, it arrives.

'Fuck if I know,' he answers.

It's that miserable rainy day again, the day I sat in the café waiting for my new boyfriend, and he came.

We're standing there, like idiots, when a tiny blonde teenage girl with a totally stressed face, comes right up to us. Says, in a Polish voice:

'Please, I look for Sam. You are his parents, yes?'

Ania

Maciek. Maciek. Maciek!

No, no, no.

Please. Please. Please.

A part of my brain listens and thinks: Isn't it strange? When all else is gone, when the day is as bad as a day can get, I find myself saying everything three times. Saying them aloud, or to myself, I have no idea. I am breathing and pleading, one two three. Rocking myself on the settee, and repeating these words. Maciek. Maciek. Maciek! No, no, no. Please. Please. Please.

I try not to cry too hard, worried about the baby. Crying is such hard work for stomach muscles. And I don't want my panic to drip into the baby's world. It is my pain, and I try to keep it separate.

Ian is so sweet. He's puzzled, because Maciek is only a man who fixed our central heating, but he comforts me just the same. How can he compete with a dying lover? He puts his arms around me and I let him hold me. This doesn't help. He is the wrong shape. His are the wrong hands.

MAY

Evanton

May is yellow-flowered and fickle, and far more cruel than April. Hail storms ruin picnics on the beach, clothes hung on lines get drenched by sudden squalls: but no one can bring themselves to utterly distrust May. Soft southerly winds stir old memories and saps rise even in the most jaded hearts.

The days stretch on and on, with children needing to be called in to bed, while the sky is still excitingly blue. Babies and old people wake at 4am to skylarks and sea gulls. By afternoon, everyone in Evanton is flagging, only to find the light pulling them out of doors again after dinner. Babies are born, and these spring babies are different from winter babies. All their lives, they expect life to be full of light.

Ania struggles with her son's hunger, while Ian reads On Chesil Beach. *Everything in Ian's world has shifted, since the birth. It's a wonder no one has reported this at school, that their teacher is entirely a stranger. Everything is different, everything is new. He puts down his book, smiles and sits on their bed. With his fingers, he guides the nipple home. How does he know how to do this? But he does.*

Ania blows an absentminded kiss to her husband when Mikolaj finally latches on. Ian is like someone she hardly knows, or used to know when she was a kid. He inspires a stirring affection, a faint connection, but still he is oddly irrelevant. As is everyone these days. Then she stares at her new son, unused yet to the fact of him. This is what the bump has amounted to! As proper a human being as anybody. She cannot imagine not wanting to stare at him, to stroke his head.

Mikolaj, of course, concentrates on food. He sucks and sucks till sated, then swoons into sleep, nipple still in mouth. Ania whispers the vowels and consonants of his name like a love song, or a pining song. Like a song that ends homesickness. But it is really Maciek, she is saying, she is singing. As if, having no excuse to be on her tongue anymore, it has insinuated itself into other words.

Maciek's caravan, what is left of it, has been taken away, and though grass is already growing, the weight of the caravan has left permanent grooves in the ground. Pizza Palace has a new manager, a woman this time, someone who met Maciek once or twice but never really noticed him. She's not as good at keeping the silver tubs filled up, but the customers like her. Maciek's hand mirror is still hanging in the back room, and she uses it to check her lipstick. One thousand, five hundred and ninety-five miles away, Maciek's cardboard boxes sit in his Ciotka Agata's upstairs spare room. Inside the boxes are souvenirs of his life – old letters, diaries, photographs. Favourite books and music, old and scratched. Agata sits by the boxes, sifting through them, deciding who would like to have this or that. Hard to believe he will not walk through the door again, bringing gifts and the smell of a foreign country. Difficult to measure his absence, really; the family has been missing him since he moved away. It's another layer of missing. Agata thinks of her sister, Maciek's mother. Remembers the two of them walking in the rain to the market and swinging little Maciek between them, laughing. One, two, three, whee! And what do you think of that slut Marja dumping her rich lover and flying to the funeral? Imagine that! And she's not been seen in town since, says the gossip. Maybe she's moving to Scotland?

Rose has moved her things back into her old house on Camden Street, and is curled up in front of the fire, reading Far from the Madding Crowd. *She is frowning. Look out for Troy! she wants to warn Bathsheba. Gabriel Oak's the one!*

She reads a lot these days, has cut back on the wine. Curiously, this has not been difficult. She feels older and at ease with this, as if her heart has finally caught up with herself. As if for the last few years, she has been stalled, crashing the gears, racing the engine beyond its capacity. Whatever was wrong is over now, and she feels as lucky as if she'd been pulled from a sinking ship in a roiling sea.

Harry is dancing around their bedroom in his new boxer shorts, listening to The Rolling Stones and convincing himself that he may not have gotten all he wanted, but he's got what he needs, damn it. Heads for a bath, looks forward to his bed, and the next morning, and the next day too.

Sam and Roksana watch a DVD in his bedroom and drink Stella out of coffee mugs. Just one large bottle between them, they sip slowly to make it last. It's almost 10:30 on a school night, and they are alone in his bedroom, drinking beer. Isn't this bad? Why isn't a parent telling them to stop? Roksana smells like snowdrops, and Jake is long, long gone. Sam doesn't care that the movie is a naff girly film. His eyes graze the screen, but he's not watching the movie. Roksana is so light, she is tilted towards him on the sofa. Her body gives off a perfumed heat. Then for no reason, he thinks about the hat Maciek used to wear all the time, the beat-up old trilby. He wonders if the blast saved the hat, and even now, it is perched up in the branches of a tree. One of those tall oaks at the edge of the caravan park. Maybe right now, some bird is teasing it apart, for a nest. Or just for something to do. Leonardo pulls Kate down the grand staircase, as her fiancé fires shots at them. Sam stretches his legs, his arms. Lets them rest closer to Roksana. In his mind, climbs up into the branches of the tall oak to take down the trilby and puts it on his own head. Salutes his friend, by touching the tip of the hat and nodding, exactly the way Maciek used to. With the smile that hardly made it to his eyes. Then he kisses the side of Roksana's head so softly, at first she pretends not to notice.

The Locart Principle is simple. It says that everything and everyone leaves a trace. It's a comforting idea. Perhaps we move through time, leaving criss-crossing smears of our having been, like snails before dawn on a rain-washed pavement. Hearts stop beating, but nobody completely disappears. Evanton's houses crouch up in the shadows of hills, and from a distance seem connected. Seem to tumble together towards the shore like a single, bumbling, benevolent being. And maybe, just maybe, that applies to the inhabitants too. All the people who have been and all the people who are still here, tangled up together. Oh, the mess! On and on, a single thumping heart. Everyone dreaming and planning, as if their future happiness is a place, all shiny and bright. As if it exists already, and they just have to keep the car on the road to get there.

ACKNOWLEDGEMENTS

For inspiration, I am indebted to Alan and our maddening marriage, and to Arec Jablonski for insights into romantic melancholia. I am also, oddly, indebted to hormonal upheavals – mine and everyone else's. Thank you, storms of insanity!

For lending me the precious Leith sitting room to write in, and for the confidence-giving compliments, thank you Margaret MacPherson. And for the use of her lovely Coll house, thank you Mairi Hedderwick.

For invaluable editorial help, thank you Angus Dunn, Fee Murray and Peter Whitely. For help with research, I would have been lost without Madge Sanderson, Saskia Fraser, and the queen of libraryland Jill Merideth. A huge thank you to Ania Koskowska and Michal Koskowski, for patiently criticising my blundering assumptions about Polish culture and language.

If Sam has any credibility, it is entirely due to Nick Rogerson's astute assessment of adolescence, while being at the same time immersed in it; a rare feat.

And for the financial support making it possible to both eat and write, many thanks to the Scottish Arts Council.